Praise for
New York Times and USA Today Bestselling Author

Diane Capri

"Full of thrills and tension, but smart and human, too."
*Lee Child, #1 World Wide Bestselling Author of Jack Reacher
Thrillers*

"[A] welcome surprise….[W]orks from the first page to 'The
End'."
Larry King

"Swift pacing and ongoing suspense are always
present…[L]ikable protagonist who uses her political
connections for a good cause…Readers should eagerly anticipate
the next [book]."
Top Pick, Romantic Times

"…offers tense legal drama with courtroom overtones, twisty
plot, and loads of Florida atmosphere. Recommended."
Library Journal

"[A] fast-paced legal thriller…energetic prose…an appealing
heroine…clever and capable supporting cast…[that will] keep
readers waiting for the next [book]."
Publishers Weekly

"Expertise shines on every page."
*Margaret Maron, Edgar, Anthony, Agatha and Macavity Award
Winning MWA Past President*

LATE ARRIVAL

by DIANE CAPRI

Published by: AugustBooks
http://www.AugustBooks.com

ISBN: 978-1-942633-31-0

Original cover design by: Dar Albert
Digital formatting by: Author E.M.S.
Interior cat silhouettes used under CC0 license from openclipart.org.

Late Arrival is a work of fiction. Names, characters, places, and
incidents either are the product of the author's imagination or are used
fictitiously, and any resemblance to actual persons, living or dead,
business establishments, events, or locales is entirely coincidental.

Published in the United States of America.

Visit the author website:
http://www.DianeCapri.com

ALSO BY DIANE CAPRI

The Park Hotel Mysteries Series
Reservation with Death
Early Check Out
Room with a Clue
Late Arrival

The Hunt for Justice Series
Due Justice
Twisted Justice
Secret Justice
Wasted Justice
Raw Justice
Mistaken Justice (*novella*)
Cold Justice (*novella*)
False Justice (*novella*)
Fair Justice (*novella*)
True Justice (*novella*)
Night Justice

The Heir Hunter Series
Blood Trails
Trace Evidence

Jordan Fox Mysteries Series
False Truth
(An 11-book continuity series)

The Hunt for Jack Reacher Series:
(in publication order with Lee Child source books in parentheses)

Don't Know Jack (The Killing Floor)

Jack in a Box (*novella*)

Jack and Kill (*novella*)

Get Back Jack (Bad Luck & Trouble)

Jack in the Green (*novella*)

Jack and Joe (The Enemy)

Deep Cover Jack (Persuader)

Jack the Reaper (The Hard Way)

Black Jack (Running Blind/The Visitor)

Ten Two Jack (The Midnight Line)

Jack of Spades (Past Tense)

The Jess Kimball Thrillers Series

Fatal Enemy (*novella*)

Fatal Distraction

Fatal Demand

Fatal Error

Fatal Fall

Fatal Edge (*novella*)

Fatal Game

Fatal Bond

Fatal Past (*novella*)

Fatal Dawn

LATE
ARRIVAL

CHAPTER ONE

Dear Miss Charlotte,

Thank you so much for the pictures of your new baby grand-niece. She is beautiful. And yes, I know I'm getting older, and the baby clock is ticking, but I need to find a decent man first. And no, I'm not sending you pictures of the sheriff. I appreciate the sentiment that a rugged Texas sheriff would make a great husband, but we're just friends. I swear.

I'm hoping the next time I write I will have a new address. Living in the hotel is taking its toll, and I miss my little Scout and Jem. It's time for me to get a place of my own, and thanks to my friend June, the florist I told you about, I'll be renting her cute bungalow while she's out traveling the world. I will definitely send you pictures of the house. I think you'd love it. It's a far cry from the granite mansion you and I lived in while I was growing up.

Thank you for the invitation to spend Christmas with you and your family this year. I will definitely think on it and let you know. I have to admit I'm a bit worried about what winter is going to be like here. I have spent cold, snowy months in Michigan before, but I think living in California spoiled me.

I've had a few short conversations with Mom and Dad, but nothing unusual to report on that front, either.

As always, I miss you. And I hope to see you soon.

With all my love,

Andi

CHAPTER TWO

"YOU'VE LOST MY CLUBS. My very expensive clubs. How incompetent does a person have to be to lose something as large as a set of golf clubs?" the squat man demanded with his beady little eyes glaring at me from behind designer eyeglasses.

I stared across my concierge desk and tried really hard not to throw my silver-plated hotel pen at him. I bit my tongue to avoid reminding him that I didn't lose a damn thing that belonged to him. Nor did I say that somewhere along the way from the airport to the Park Hotel lobby, *he* was the one who had lost sight of his golf clubs. The clubs were probably still in the shuttle along with all the other oversized items the dock porters had collected at the ferry.

He'd arrived late, and he was in a hurry, and he was an impatient jerk. The fourth impatient jerk I'd dealt with today. So far.

"I'm sure, Mr. Fasco, that we will be able to locate your clubs and return them to you. As you can clearly see," I gestured to the chaotic, bustling lobby behind him, "we are trying to get all the guests checked in for the charity tournament. It's highly likely that your clubs were held up in the rush to get everyone into the hotel in an orderly manner."

Although the scene before me was the opposite of orderly. I'd call it extreme chaos. Not only were more than fifty golfers checking into the hotel for the Frontenac Island Charity Tournament all at once, but there was a kindergarten class of thirty rowdy five-year-olds roaming the corridors and the grounds for a history lesson on Frontenac Island and the Park Hotel.

Whoever had scheduled these two events simultaneously had a lot to answer for, in my humble opinion.

One of the rambunctious, mischievous students was hiding under my desk as I attempted to calm Mr. Fasco. I don't know how or when the kid got there, but currently, he was poking me in the shin and giggling. It took all I had not to kick the little scamp. Not hard, of course. I would never hurt a child. But a slight nudge with the toe of my black pump to show him who was boss wouldn't be remiss under these circumstances, surely.

This was the kind of week I was having. A swirling storm of disgruntled guests. And nothing I did seemed to be enough for any of them. I was off my game, that was for sure. I just hoped Samuel didn't notice, because this was the first week that we had implemented the two-tiered concierge system I'd argued for as a way to keep my job.

Casey Cushing, the Park's long-time concierge, had returned from his personal leave. He'd been taking care of his mother during her hip surgery and subsequent recovery for the past few months. While I was on the desk today, he was helping Ginny with organizing and executing the week's events at the Park

Hotel. We alternated weeks at the desk and helping with events. My bad luck plopped me on the desk during one of our busiest times of the year.

Every late September, the Park Hotel hosted a charity golf tournament for the CEOs of Michigan's prominent businesses. It was a chance for them to use the hotel to mingle and talk shop and raise money for their own charitable causes. The tournament was a terrific event that benefited programs catering to those in need, like Habitat for Humanity Detroit and the Hope Network. But some of the CEOs were far from easy to please.

Case in point...

Mr. Fasco sucked on his teeth, which desperately needed some chemical whitening, and was as petulant as the five-year-old under my desk. He said, "I don't care about anyone else. My clubs are worth more than you make in a month. I will sue this hotel if my clubs are lost or stolen. Which is a high possibility by the looks of your porters."

I bit my tongue, almost to the point of making it bleed. The man was plain rude as well as dead wrong. All of our porters were fine people and excellent at their jobs, as was everyone else employed by the Park Hotel. They wouldn't be working here otherwise. Several of our porters were of Ojibwa descent. Our newest porter, Josh Smallwood, was the eighteen-year-old cousin of Tina, one of our most experienced members of the Chamber Crew. I'd spotted Josh hustling his butt off, carrying in several loads of luggage from the horse-drawn shuttles parked out front. He'd been working eight hours straight without a break—and without complaint. Unlike some people who wouldn't lift a travel bag at gunpoint.

"I'm sorry for the inconvenience, Mr. Fasco," I said as sweetly as I could and slid a piece of paper toward him along with my pen. "Please write down a description of your golf bag and clubs, and when we locate them, I'll call you and have them sent to your suite."

"You'll recognize my bag immediately. My name tag is attached to the handle." Sneering, he picked up the pen and scrawled a brief description of his designer bag and clubs. He mumbled under his breath as he wrote. I picked out a few words that I didn't care to repeat or acknowledge.

As soon as he finished, a harried young woman wearing a gray pantsuit strolled up behind Mr. Fasco, rolling a set of golf clubs behind her. "Mr. Fasco, I found your clubs."

He whirled around. "For Pete's sake, Melanie. Don't ever sneak up on me like that."

"Sorry, sir, but I found your clubs."

"Where were they?"

"In the shuttle, sir."

When Mr. Fasco turned back to me, I gave him one of my thin *I'm barely preventing myself from smacking you* smiles. "Well, look at that."

He rolled his eyes. "My assistant is so disorganized."

The hapless Melanie's eyes widened, but she didn't argue.

I replied, "But she did find your clubs, so there is that."

He glared at me, pushed his pricey glasses up onto his nose, turned, and walked away. He barked at Melanie, "Come on. We need to sign in for the tournament. At least this foolishness with my clubs didn't delay us too long."

Before Melanie scampered off behind her boss, I waved her over. "I'm so sorry about all of this. I'm sure Mr. Fasco's under a lot of stress."

She exhaled a long breath. "Don't apologize for him. He's a real peach whether he's stressed or not."

She didn't need to say more. I recognized the ambitious look in her eyes. She was assistant to Mr. Fasco for now, but the job wouldn't last forever. She was going places, and she wouldn't let a jerk like Mr. Fasco interfere with her upward mobility. She'd do what she had to do to get herself ahead. I had to admire her pluck.

"What room are you in?" I asked.

"Room 236."

"Charge your food and beverages to your room. I'll make sure the bills get comped. Working for Mr. Fasco, you'll more than earn free food and booze all weekend, I'd say."

She gave me a huge grin. "Thank you. You may have saved my life."

I nodded. "I aim to please."

When she left, I inhaled deeply and focused on the next problem. I looked down at the little face staring up at me with a goofy, gap-toothed smile.

"Okay, little man, time to deal with you."

He folded his hands together as if in prayer. "Don't rat me out. Please. I can't go back—I just can't."

I suppressed a grin. "Why not? What's the problem?"

"It's Lexi. She wants to kiss me."

His confession lifted my eyebrows. Five-year-olds were kissing now? "Oh. I see. That *is* a problem. You don't want Lexi to kiss you?"

He shook his head vehemently. "Kissing is gross."

"Okay, well, the best thing you can do is to tell Lexi not to kiss you. Tell her you don't like it."

"What if she doesn't listen?"

"Then you need to tell your teacher. You should never let anyone do things to you that you don't want."

His face scrunched up like he was thinking about it. "And that will work?"

"Yes."

"Okay." He crawled out from under my desk and offered his hand. "Thank you for helping me. You are very nice."

"You are most welcome, little man." I took his small hand and shook it. "Now, we should find your teacher. She's probably worried about you."

No sooner had I said that than a frantic-looking woman with steel-gray hair came charging through the lobby.

I waved her over. "I think I have what you're looking for." I led the boy around the concierge desk.

She dropped to her knees and hugged him. "Manuel. You had us all worried." Then she looked up at me. "Thank you for finding him."

"No problem. He was no trouble." I winked at him.

He smiled and took his teacher's hand as they left.

One more crisis averted. I checked it off my list. I felt like I needed a high-five or something. As I went back around my desk, my cell phone buzzed. I took it out of my pocket and saw a text from Daniel.

Date night? I'm on the island for a meeting with the mayor.

I texted back: *Can't tonight. Got a bachelorette party to go to. One of the girls from the hotel is getting married.*

He wrote: *Call me later when you're tipsy. I can stay over. (kissy face emoji)*

Maybe, if you're lucky, I texted with a big grin on my face. My cheeks flushed.

I was taking a huge step here, having kept Daniel at a safe distance. I kind of left him hanging, quite literally, the night my suite was trashed. I'd been contemplating ending our blossoming

relationship because of my conflicted feelings for Sheriff Luke
Jackson. Feelings that I had since managed to squelch. The
sheriff and I just weren't going to happen. We had a strong
friendship, a mutually respectful working relationship, and I
didn't want to ruin that.

I figured he felt the same way, because I'd only seen him
twice since the break-in. Once to update me. He'd said lots of
fingerprints had been found, which wasn't surprising. I lived in a
hotel, after all. There'd been no matches in the criminal database
systems. My laptop, which had been stolen, hadn't turned up at
the local pawn shop. No surprise there, either. The other time I'd
seen him was when he came to the hotel to take his daughter
Megan, who worked here, out to lunch for her birthday.

There'd been no phone calls from the sheriff. Not that I
expected any.

The break-in had rattled me in more ways than one. The
sheriff and I had nearly kissed during a weak moment for both of
us. We'd been dealing with the stress of solving a murder, on top
of the reality that my suite had been destroyed by someone
looking for something, and I still had no clue what it could have
been.

I'd moved into another suite while mine was repaired.
Recently, I'd moved back, but I didn't want to live at the hotel
anymore. A serendipitous opportunity had come up. I would be
moving into a little house in the village soon. My cats, Scout and
Jem, would be ecstatic. I missed them terribly, and they were
restless and bored living apart from me, too.

"Only three more hours to go, then it's drinking time,"
Ginny Park said.

Momentarily startled, I looked up to see my best friend
smiling at me across the desk. She was trying a new hairstyle.

Two little buns were perched on the sides of her head, like misplaced earmuffs. She looked like a hippie Princess Leia. Not entirely a bad look for her, to be honest. She was so adorable that she could pull off just about any style.

"How crazy is this pre-wedding thing going to get, do you think?" I wasn't a big drinker or partier, so I was more than a bit apprehensive. A small room filled with drunken revelers didn't sound like my idea of a great time.

"Do you remember that kegger Jessica hosted during our second year in college where that guy, Craig, wrapped himself in toilet paper and ran through the dorm screaming that he was a mummy?"

I nodded. "Yeah?"

"It'll be just like that. But without any toilet-paper mummies. Or Craig." She shrugged. "Well, I'm not sure I can promise that, really. But it'll be fun. You'll see."

I was skeptical. The party would be held in the pub at the clubhouse on the golf course that was part of the hotel grounds. As far as I'd heard, almost every woman within a five-mile radius planned to be there. That's just how it was in a small community. Everybody knew everybody. I'd been learning that living on an island had its challenges as well as its rewards.

Sometimes the "challenges" side of the scale was a little bit heavier, though, as I would soon find out yet again.

CHAPTER THREE

THE NOISE WAS NEARLY deafening inside the pub at the clubhouse. The body heat from sixty loud, sweaty women crammed together, drinking and talking and laughing, hung over me, sticky and cloying. Sweat rolled down my back and slicked my face.

None of this seemed to bother Ginny. Tendrils of hair stuck to her flushed cheeks as she downed yet another tequila shot in one gulp.

She slammed the shot glass down onto the table with gusto, rattling all the empty glasses already gathered there. Then she threw up her hands and cheered. Everyone around our table took up the cheer, and it spread through the entire place. The nonstop cacophony of celebration continued as everyone downed shots in honor of the bride and the wedding and anything else people could think of.

Ginny threw her arm around me and leaned into my ear. "Are you having fun?"

I lifted my first gin and tonic, which I was sipping slowly. "Yes."

Her eyes narrowed. "Then finish that drink and have a shot with me."

I took a sip, and she put her finger on the bottom of the glass and tilted it up so I'd drink more. I drained the glass and set it down with force. "There. Happy?"

"Even Mom is having a good time." She gestured to the small karaoke stage where Lois and the bride-to-be, Tina, were singing along to the music with style and heart. I had no idea Lois could shake her hips so robustly.

"She deserves to let loose and have some fun," I said.

Ginny nodded. "I worry about her."

I knew she was referring to the occasions where she'd come across Lois talking to her dead husband, Henry. I'd witnessed it myself. At first, it didn't worry me—lots of people talk to their deceased loved ones for comfort. But Lois seemed convinced that Henry was still here. In the hotel. She would use conversations she'd had with Henry to justify her decisions, too. When she wanted to implement a change, sometimes she would say, "Henry wants it that way." She'd actually used "Henry's wishes" to persuade Samuel not to fire me.

"She'll be okay. There's been a lot of stress at the hotel lately. It's just her way of dealing with things," I said.

"I'm not sure it's the healthiest way, though. I really worry about her mental health if she keeps this up. She's almost delusional about it." She looked down at the table and fiddled with an empty shot glass.

I didn't want her to be sad. I nudged her shoulder. "She's tough. I've never known a stronger woman than Lois."

"That's true." She gave me a little smile.

"I thought we were going to do shots?"

She threw her arm into the air. "Yes! Finally! Andi Steele is going to have some fun."

"Hey, now. Don't be mean." I laughed.

She handed me a shot of tequila. I took the glass, resigned to drink it, but I wasn't a very good drinker. Together we salted our hands, licked the salt, tossed the alcohol back, and sucked on a lime. I grimaced the whole way through. Tequila was an acquired taste, and I had never acquired it. Nor did I really want to. Ginny, on the other hand, could drink tequila like water.

After another shot, I was feeling no pain. My body was extremely relaxed. Maybe too relaxed. I was having trouble sitting erect on my stool. I had to lean on the table a little to keep my balance. What a lightweight.

"I want to fall in love," Ginny said dreamily. "No." She slapped her hand down. "I want someone to sweep me off my feet. I deserve to be swept away. I want a sweeper!"

"I agree." That was one area in life where Ginny never seemed to be lucky—love. Not that I was any luckier. I'd had two serious relationships in my life, and both ended poorly. I had a knack for choosing the wrong men.

"Clinton's not a sweeper." She shook her head as she discussed her current boyfriend. "He's not very ambitious." She looked at me, narrowed her eyes. "Do you think Daniel's a sweeper?"

If he was, he hadn't managed to do it for me. To be fair, maybe it was because I wouldn't let him.

Ginny made a face and slapped me on the arm. "You know who I bet is a sweeper? The sheriff." She wriggled her eyebrows at me. "I could picture that man lifting a woman without any effort right into his arms and carrying her away to some isolated cabin in the woods. He's definitely a woodsy man and not a beachy man. I'll bet he'd be ravaging her for days upon days."

I swallowed. She was right. I could picture the sheriff doing that, too.

"What about Clive Barrington?" I teased her. "I'll bet he's got what it takes to be a sweeper. Did you see those biceps?"

"Whew," Ginny said, laughing as she wiped her brow. "It's warm in here. I need some water. Do you want some water?"

"Yes, please."

While Ginny pushed her way to the bar to get two glasses of water, the sheriff's daughter Megan, who worked with the bride as one of the cleaning crew, stumbled out of nowhere and wrapped an arm around me. She was very drunk and could barely stand.

"Andi," she breathed into my face. The alcoholic fumes were nearly suffocating. If I lit a match, I'd probably blow the place up.

"Hey, Megan. You all right?"

"I'm goooooooooood." She laughed. Then she looked soberly at me, her brow furrowed into thinking lines. "Did you break my dad's heart?"

"Um, no." I fidgeted in my chair.

"I think you did. He's so damn moody. I mean, he's always been moody, but this…this is different. I've never seen him like this. Well, maybe once before when Mom left him."

I patted her hand. "I assure you, I did not break your dad's heart."

She stared at me for a long moment. "He likes you, you know. Like, *likes* you. You know what I mean?"

"I know what you mean."

"Do you like him?"

I licked my lips, thinking about my answer. Should I lie to her? I could tell her the truth, get it out in the open, and she'd never remember it anyway since she was so drunk. Maybe I could unburden myself...all I'd have to do is confess it out loud.

I opened my mouth, but before I could say anything, a thumping dance song came on, and Megan began jumping up and down. "I love this song!" Then she gyrated through the crowd away from me.

When Ginny came back with the water, I nearly chugged the whole glass in one long gulp.

The party wound down about one in the morning, and the majority of the partiers streamed out of the pub. There were several hotel golf carts with drivers waiting for those who wanted or needed a ride home. Lois had arranged all of this for Tina, the bride-to-be. Because Tina worked at the Park. And because we all liked Tina. That was one of the things I loved about this island, this village. Everyone looked out for each other.

Ginny and I opted to walk together back to the hotel. I told her I'd spend the night at her suite, instead of going back to mine alone. I didn't want to admit it, but I was afraid to be alone in my suite, especially at night. The break-in still haunted me. If it had been a random burglary, maybe I'd have been able to relax. But I'd been targeted, watched, victimized, and I still didn't know why or by whom.

We walked arm in arm down the picturesque path that dissected the golf course from the hotel. It wasn't a long walk. We enjoyed the unusually warm September evening. Ginny said it wouldn't be too long before snow started to fall. Which was something I wasn't looking forward to. I dreaded the coming Michigan winter. I'd lived through a few while I was in college in Ann Arbor and never learned to enjoy the snow.

"You know what I really want," Ginny said. "I want to travel."

"Like to Mexico or somewhere warm?" I shivered a little in my sweater.

"Maybe, but I mean really travel. Like to Europe or Australia or Africa, even. For a few months. Maybe a whole year."

"Really? I never heard you say that before. I always thought you wanted to find a man and settle down with a passel of kids."

She shook her head. "Nope. That's what my mom wants me to do. She'd be happy if I never left home again. But that's not what I truly want." She gripped my arm tight. "Could you imagine strolling down the streets of Paris? Having breakfast at a little café, flirting a little with the adorable French waiter. Maybe spending the day at the Louvre, or up in the Eiffel Tower, or a night at the Moulin Rouge." She smiled dreamily. "Could you imagine?"

"And a gorgeous French man would sweep you off your feet, I assume?" I smiled.

"Yes!" She squeezed my arm again and giggled.

"What's stopping you?"

"Everything. Mom, my job at the hotel, money…"

"Money? What kind of money problems could you possibly have? You'll inherit a fortune one day," I said, squeezing her arm.

She shook her head. "Not unless we sold the Park. Which none of us would ever do. As long as we can keep the old place going, we will. Too many people here depend on us for their livelihoods, you know?"

Her wistfulness caught me unaware. The Park family never seemed to want for anything. But I hadn't considered that the equity in the historic hotel was not the same as cash in the bank.

We walked a few more steps in silence before I said, "If you really want to travel, find a way. Life is way too short to have big regrets like that."

She nodded. "Yeah. You're right. I'm going to do it. I'll find a way to do it." She let my arm go and ran out onto the golf course.

"Where are you going?"

"I have to pee," she said, laughing and hopping from one foot to another.

"You can't hold it until we get to the hotel?" But she was already too far upwind to hear me.

She jogged a little ways and then ducked behind some bushes.

Shaking my head, I wandered over to a pretty wooden bench near a copse of trees just off the path to wait for her. While I sat there, I felt the shadows closing in on me. A sudden creeping sensation took hold. I shook it off.

"Hurry, Gin. It's getting cold out here."

"Just give me a minute!" she shouted and then giggled.

I rubbed my hands up and down my arms, unable to warm away the chills. It almost felt like I was being watched. I looked around. I was alone in this section of the course. There was a group of three women about fifty feet away, heading toward the hotel. Their laughter carried across the grass. It should've made me feel better, more secure, but it didn't.

I turned toward the bushes. "Ginny! C'mon!"

A shiver raced down my back—something wasn't right. I stood up just as a wide hand clamped down around my right wrist and swung me backward toward one of the trees. On instinct, I reacted and lashed out. Without really seeing who had attacked me, I struck toward the face and throat with my left hand, hoping to connect with something. I kicked out with my leg, aiming for his groin. I was rewarded with a hard grunt, and the hand on my wrist dropped away.

It was then I saw who had grabbed me, and the blood drained from my face. Even in the moonlit night, I recognized his features. I felt woozy. I reached out and pressed my hand against the closest tree so I didn't fall to the ground.

He looked the same, except his hair was a bit longer and there was a little gray peppered in with the dark. Stubble marred his usually clean-shaven chin as he rubbed the spot where I'd hit him.

"Jeremy?"

His face tilted toward me, and he smiled. "Hey, Andi."

CHAPTER FOUR

HE STRAIGHTENED, AND I noticed he favored his leg a little. That was where I must've kicked him, narrowly missing his groin. "Is that any way to greet a friend?"

He certainly wasn't a friend. He was Jeremy Rucker, my old boss. The one who had embezzled millions from our firm's clients and left me holding the bag. He was directly responsible for the situation I found myself in now. No way to practice law any more in California or anywhere else. Working as a concierge at the Park Hotel.

Come to think of it, maybe I should've given him a few more kicks for good measure.

"What are you doing here?"

"I thought I'd surprise you."

I shook my head, which was still a little swimmy from the tequila and the shock of seeing Jeremy. "How can you even be here? What about your bail conditions? Surely, you're not allowed to leave the state of California before the trial."

"Don't worry about that. I got it all worked out."

I looked him over, shocked to see him walking free right here on Frontenac Island. He'd tried to hit the road once already, but the firm had tracked him down. He'd been caught at the airport in Maui, about to board a plane to Tahiti. The courts had shipped him back to California for trial. I'd thought I might have had to testify in court, but the firm's criminal lawyers said my testimony wasn't necessary. I didn't know anything about Jeremy's embezzling, anyway.

Ginny had stumbled over to where we stood. "What's going on? Who's this?"

"This is Jeremy Rucker."

Her eyes widened. "*The* Jeremy? Your ex-boss? The embezzler?"

"Alleged embezzler," he said like any good criminal lawyer might have. "They haven't proved anything yet."

"Why are you here?" I asked coldly.

"To see you, of course."

Anger clipped my voice. He was not being straight with me. No surprise there. Jeremy had proved to be an excellent liar. "And how did you find me here?"

He sighed, rubbing at his chin again. I wondered if I'd really punched him hard enough to justify his theatrics. I hoped so. He deserved as much…and more. "You'd be surprised how easy it is to get information out of people, especially in a small town like this one."

True. Hadn't the town's penchant for gossip been my biggest asset when I was investigating those murders? Everyone seemed to know everything about everybody around here, and they were all more than willing to share.

"Everyone was talking about the bachelorette party at the clubhouse." He glanced at Ginny. "You aren't the bride-to-be, are you?"

"No," Ginny said.

He narrowed his eyes and pointed a finger at her. "No, wait...I know who you are. Ginny Park. You went to college with Andi, didn't you? I recognize you from your picture."

"What do you want, Jeremy?"

"I need something."

I frowned. "What could you possibly need from me?"

"You have a flash drive that belongs to me."

My frown deepened. "I don't have anything that's yours. Why would you say that?"

"Don't mess around with me, Andi. I really need that drive." He took a step closer.

Ginny piped up. "Hey, she said she doesn't know what you're talking about."

He turned his head toward Ginny, and I didn't like the way he looked at her. Like she was disposable. I had to diffuse the situation I felt building. "Jeremy, I'm telling you that I don't have a flash drive that belongs to you."

He sighed again, clenching his jaw. "You might not know you have it."

"What do you mean?"

"I put it in—"

"What's going on?" Daniel stepped out of the dark and onto the path.

Jeremy took a visible step away from me and unclenched his fists. "Hey, nothing's going on, buddy. I'm just talking to an old friend."

Daniel looked at me. "Andi, are you okay?"

"I'm fine, Daniel."

Ginny wasn't having it. "This is Jeremy Rucker. He was threatening Andi."

"Ginny," I warned.

"Well, he was."

Daniel moved closer, standing between Jeremy and me. "I suggest you walk away, *buddy*."

Jeremy looked at me, then Daniel. I could tell he was sizing up the situation. Jeremy had been an affable man to work for. I'd never felt uneasy around him. He'd never hit on me, except one time when he was really drunk at a staff party, which didn't really count. I'd never seen him become uncontrollably angry. He'd always seemed so even tempered. Until now. Now I felt a perceptible level of violence wafting off him like an icy breeze off the lake.

He put his hands up and backed away. "Okay, okay. I don't want any problems."

Daniel lowered his guard a little and glanced over his shoulder at me. That was a mistake. Jeremy took a swing at him. Daniel leaned away and avoided Jeremy's fist. Then he stepped forward and struck Jeremy hard on the chin with an uppercut, like a man accustomed to fighting. Jeremy stumbled to the side. He spat blood out onto the grass. He must've bitten his lip or tongue from the solid punch.

"You'll regret that," he said, wiping the blood away with the back of his hand.

"Never come near Andi again." Daniel's voice was ice cold. I'd never heard him speak like that before.

Jeremy spat another glob of blood and saliva on the ground before he turned and disappeared into the trees lining the pathway on the golf course.

I didn't realize how much I'd been shaking until Daniel wrapped his arms around me and pulled me into the warmth and solidness of his chest. "Are you okay?"

I nodded, even as my teeth chattered.

Ginny plowed into us from the side, wrapping her arms around us both. "Hug me. I was so scared."

I disentangled my arm that was trapped between her and Daniel's and wrapped it around her shoulders. Daniel did the same, and we hugged her tight.

A flash of light swept over us. I lifted my head to see Sheriff Jackson brandishing a flashlight, his other hand dangerously close to his holster.

He said, "I heard there was a fight going on."

Daniel and I broke away, but Ginny still clung to me.

"Some guy attacked Andi," Daniel said.

The sheriff's gaze moved toward me with his usual curiosity, but there was something else there. Concern. I nodded. "It was Jeremy Rucker."

The sheriff frowned. "Your ex-boss?"

"Yeah. I don't know what he was doing here. He must have skipped bail or something. I think his trial's coming up soon, so they'll be looking for him."

Sheriff Jackson turned off his flashlight and slid it back into his utility belt. He took out the notebook he always carried. "All right, let's hear the details."

With a promise to put a call in to authorities in California, the sheriff let us go an hour later. Ginny walked with him, and I walked with Daniel. The event had sobered me up, to be sure, but I still didn't feel very well. The world was still a bit spinny. Without any words, I stumbled through the door of my suite and collapsed onto the bed. Daniel hovered on the steps.

"I can crash on the sofa," he said.

I lifted my arm up toward him and wriggled my fingers. He came to the bed, nuzzled in behind me, and wrapped an arm around me.

Sighing, I leaned back into him. I hadn't been held like this in more years than I wanted to admit. "How did you know where to find me?"

"You texted me and told me to come get you at the clubhouse.

I frowned. "Really? God, I don't remember that at all."

"I had a feeling you were very drunk. Your spelling was horrendous. And you're usually a stickler for grammar in your texts."

I could feel him smiling. "Well, I'm glad you were able to decipher my gibberish."

"Me, too." He pressed his hand against my belly, and little licks of heat cascaded up my body. "Are you sure you're okay?"

I nodded. "He just scared me a little."

"The sheriff seemed to know who he was."

I sighed, too tired to soothe Daniel's ego. I grabbed his hand and brought it up to my chest, holding it tight. "I'm tired. I'm going to sleep."

CHAPTER FIVE

WHEN I WOKE UP, I rolled onto my back and smacked my lips.
I felt really weird and out of sorts as if a bad dream still lingered
on the edge of my mind. My body ached, especially my arms.
I felt like I'd done twenty laps in the pool. I wished my cats
were here. They would cuddle up with me, and we'd go back to
sleep.

Then I remembered Daniel. I patted the bed next to me.
The spot was empty and cold. I sat up, head pounding, and got
gently to my feet. I stumbled into the tiny kitchenette, hoping
there was a pot of coffee waiting for me, all hot and full of
caffeine.

"Daniel?" I turned and looked into the living room. He
wasn't there. But I did spy a note on the counter right beside a
freshly brewed pot of coffee. I smiled. *Yes, prayers answered.*
After I poured a big mug full of the aromatic brew, I read the
note.

Had to go. Meeting this afternoon. Call me later. Take two Tylenol and drink lots of coffee.
XOXO
Daniel

I swallowed the delicious caffeine and moved slowly into the bathroom to get the pain meds. I took two capsules and carried my coffee back into the bedroom, hoping for another hour's sleep before work. My cell phone buzzed from the side table.

I picked it up to see a text from Ginny.

Will you make it for the cruise? Or should I ask Casey to do it?

It was already eight o'clock. The cruise was scheduled for nine thirty. Time to get my butt in gear. I texted back—*I'll be there*—and dropped the phone on the bed.

I would not allow Casey to get all the glory. The cruise was important for the hotel. Something I had organized for the tournament weekend. I'd planned a welcome brunch on the ferry where the directors of important charities could mingle with the captains of industry. A good way to bring the money together for important causes.

I downed the coffee and rushed into the bathroom to shower. The hot water cascaded over me and washed away my fatigue and the clinging disquiet over last night's encounter with Jeremy.

Simply seeing him again had shaken me. And I had no idea what flash drive he was talking about. In all the years we'd worked together, he'd never given me a flash drive to keep for any reason.

All of the firm's client matters and accounts were maintained on shared company computers and backed up to a cloud system owned and maintained by the firm. Whatever the flash drive had on it must have been vital to him. Perhaps its contents were important to the embezzlement charges he was facing. Maybe it even contained something that would exonerate him. I shuddered when I thought that the information on that flash drive might also send him to prison for a very long time.

Whatever the flash drive was about, I still didn't have it and didn't know what was on it. Ruminating about the facts wouldn't change them. And I was running late.

I dressed, grabbed a banana for breakfast, and speed-walked down the long corridor to the main lobby of the hotel. I'd made it just in time, as Lois and Ginny were getting the stragglers organized.

When Ginny spotted me, she came over and gave my hand a squeeze. "How are you feeling?"

"Hungover." I smiled. "But I'll live."

"Are you sure? I told Lois what happened. She's very concerned. Everyone would totally understand if you wanted to take the day off."

I shook my head. "Nope. Jeremy's already stolen a lot from me. I'm not letting him take anything else. I got this."

"Okay." She squeezed my hand again.

After we got everyone wrangled up, we piled into a couple of shuttle wagons and rode down to the ferry dock. Reggie's son-in-law, Lonnie, drove one of the ferry boats that took people out onto the lake for a cruise around the island. There were several points of interest along the way. Some inlets had beautiful rock formations chiseled by glaciers, where birds and waterfowl nested. Fort Frontenac was built in 1815 as part of the fur trade and was now a historical museum. There were two lighthouses and magnificent views of the Mackinaw Bridge that connected Michigan's upper and lower peninsulas across the Straits of Mackinac.

As we set sail, I made sure the food was out and the mimosas were flowing. Servers dressed in stark black and white made their way around the two levels of the ferry, offering mini smoked salmon cupcakes, mini quiche Lorraine, and tiny stacks of blueberry pancakes. I managed to snag some of those along the way.

Ginny was the one who made everything run smoothly. My job was simply to answer questions about the island and the hotel after our guide explained the sights. I stood on the upper deck and looked out at the water and the beauty of the island as we came around the west bluff jutting out near the Park Hotel. I didn't often get to see the hotel from this vantage point. It was as breathtaking as the first day I'd crossed the lake to my new home.

Lonnie steered the ferry into the inlet as close as he could get to the shoreline below the west bluff. There was a rocky beach, currently home to a family of swans. A few mallards were spotted near the shoreline.

Stuart Minsky, the CEO of one of the biggest manufacturing companies, joined me at the railing. I'd read the biographies for all the bigwigs before the tournament and committed their names and faces to memory.

He said, "I heard there is tremendous fishing here off the island."

"Absolutely. Some of the best freshwater fish you can catch. I'd be happy to organize a charter fishing trip for you and a few of the others."

He nodded. "That sounds great."

"I'll set things up for the day after the tournament." I smiled at him. "What room are you in, Mr. Minsky?"

"I'm in the Rose Suite."

"I'll contact your assistant with the details. Cheryl, was it?"

He nodded, took out a cigar, bit off the tip, and lit the end with a gold lighter. "You are a very resourceful woman, Ms. Steele." He walked away, puffing on his cigar.

When he left, I stared out at the shoreline again. I didn't think I'd ever get tired of this view. As we edged in closer, I spotted something dark lying on the edge of the rocky shore. A large mass. It almost looked like a duffel bag or something similar.

Then I heard a gasp from someone below deck.

Lonnie slowed the boat and reversed the thrusters to hold it in relatively shallow water closer to the beach. A few minutes later, he turned the boat to return to the docks.

I squinted toward shore. My stomach started to churn and roil. I suspected what we were looking at.

There was another gasp. More voices floated around me.

"What is that?"

"Maybe it's a blanket left on the beach."

"No, I think it's…"

"Oh God, it's a…"

It was a body. And the sinking feeling in the pit of my stomach said I knew who it was.

CHAPTER SIX

AFTER THE SHERIFF AND his deputies came aboard and
interviewed everyone, he asked me to accompany him to the
beach to identify the body, since I'd told him I might know who
it was.

Lois and Ginny made sure everyone remained calm on the
boat. The most asked question was, "Would the tournament still
go on?" Lois assured everyone that it indeed would go on as
planned, which eased everyone's concerns. It was a fund-raiser,
after all.

Sheriff Jackson and I walked along the dock to his SUV. He
drove to the area of the rocky beach and parked behind the
ambulance that was already there. We stepped carefully at a slow
pace, so we wouldn't slip. Dr. Neumann, the county coroner,
walked behind us. A couple of EMTs with a body bag and
gurney followed as well.

We walked in silence. I wasn't sure what any of us
could say. It really wasn't a small-talk type of situation.

When we reached the body, the sheriff took some pictures of the twisted form. The man's leg was up near his bashed-in head.

After preliminary photos were taken of the body, the immediate area, and up at the bluff, the EMTs moved the body so it was face up. I stared at him in horror. Some of his features were unrecognizable after the fall from the bluff, but one blue eye, swaths of dark hair with that salt and pepper along the sides, and the dark stubble across his chin remained. He was still wearing the clothes he'd worn the night before.

"Can you identify him?" Sheriff Jackson asked.

"It's Jeremy Rucker." My voice shook a little.

"Okay." He put a hand on my shoulder, rubbing his thumb back and forth in a soothing manner, and then nodded at the doctor.

Dr. Neumann snapped her gloves in place and crouched to examine the body. She glanced up at the bluff and then stood. "Looks like he fell from above. Severe injuries are consistent with a fall from that height. His neck looks broken. Can't say more than that until an autopsy is completed."

His neck was broken all right. Several other bones were broken, too. It was too gruesome to look at any longer, and I turned away.

As the EMTs lifted his body, the sheriff took my arm and led me away from the scene back to the SUV. "I'm going to need you to come to the station to answer some questions. It'll be easier to get all the pertinent information that way."

"Did you call California?"

"Earlier this morning. Yeah, he definitely violated the terms of his bail. He wasn't supposed to leave the state, and there was no special arrangement or anything like that."

I rubbed my hands over my face. "I can't believe this. It's a nightmare."

He drove us over to the station and then put me in the witness room with a cup of coffee and an apple strudel from the Weiss Strudel House. They were my favorite, but I didn't know if he'd known that or if he just happened to have some apple strudel hanging around the station. Which was possible since the bakery was just down the street.

I sagged against the sofa and drank the coffee. I was thankful the sheriff didn't use an interrogation room if he didn't have to. For most interviews, he liked to use this room, with bright colors and a comfortable sofa and chair opposite a nice wooden table. There definitely was a gray sterile, one-way mirror room in the station, but for most island residents, the more comfortable room sufficed.

After about ten minutes, Sheriff Jackson came in with the notebook he always carried. He sat in the chair and put his coffee down on the table.

"I have to inform you that this interview is being recorded."

I glanced at the camera on a tripod in the corner. The little red light blinked. "Is this a formal interview?" I asked, concern starting to grow in my belly.

"Yes." He licked his lips, and I could see that this was difficult for him. "You were one of the last people to see Jeremy Rucker alive, as far as we know."

I nodded. "Okay. Let's do it." I tried to keep the irritation out of my voice, but I saw I'd failed by the wincing look the sheriff gave me. This was technically the first official interview I'd had with him. After all we'd been through on other cases, this was the first time he'd treated me like a possible suspect. It didn't feel good.

"Please state your name and address for the record."

"Andrea Steele, suite 118, the Park Hotel, Frontenac Island, Michigan."

"Could you tell me how you knew the deceased, Jeremy Rucker?"

"We used to work together at Alcott, Chambers & Rucker, a law firm in Sacramento, California. Jeremy Rucker was one of the partners of the firm and my boss."

"You left the firm in February of this year?" he asked as if he already knew the answers to these questions, because he did.

"That's right. Jeremy was arrested for embezzlement of client funds. The remaining partners thought it was best that I also step away. I was suspended, basically." It still stung when I said that out loud or even when I thought about how unfair the whole thing had been.

"When did you move to Frontenac Island?"

"End of March."

"Why did you move?"

"Because I didn't really have any other options, and Ginny Park offered me a job and a place to stay." I set my coffee cup on the table because my hands weren't as steady as I wanted them to be. The sheriff's questions were starting to worry me.

"Ginny Park, a college friend whose family owns the Park Hotel?"

"That's right." I eyed him as he scribbled in his notebook. His hair was in disarray like he'd run his hands through it a million times already today. He didn't look his usual put-together self. "I thought you were going to ask me about Jeremy?"

"I will."

"But you want to establish my possible motivation first."

His unflinching gaze met mine. "When and where was the last time you saw Jeremy Rucker before his body was discovered on the beach beneath the west bluff?"

"Last night...well, early this morning, not sure of the exact time. At the golf course just outside the clubhouse on the path to the hotel. You'd know because you were there."

"That would've been around 1:15 a.m."

I gestured. "There you go."

"Before that, when was the last time you'd seen Jeremy Rucker?"

I narrowed my gaze and sat up a little straighter in the chair. "In February, three days before he was arrested for embezzlement."

"You didn't see him after you left the firm?"

"No." It was uncomfortably warm in the room. I had to refrain from fanning my face. I didn't want him to know I was feeling uneasy.

"Did you have any contact with Mr. Rucker after February?"

"He called me once right after I moved here. In April. To apologize."

"For?"

"For being a jackass." I rubbed at my nose. "He said he was sorry that his behavior resulted in me being suspended and all that mess."

"Anything else?"

"He sent me some flowers a couple of months ago."

His eyebrows went up. "He sent you flowers? Why would he do that?"

"I have no idea."

"Was there a card with it?"

I swallowed. "Yes. It said, *See you soon.*"

He leaned forward in his chair. "So you knew he was coming to the island?"

"No. I had no idea. I just thought it was a strange message at the time."

Sheriff Jackson nodded. "When you saw him last night, what did he want?"

"He said I had something that belonged to him. A flash drive."

The sheriff frowned. "A flash drive? What's on it?"

"I have no idea because I don't have his flash drive or any flash drive." I couldn't remember the last time I'd even used a flash drive. College, maybe? My laptop didn't even have a USB port to insert a flash drive—I used cloud storage for my personal files.

"Was Jeremy Rucker the one who broke into your suite a few weeks ago?" he asked.

"How would I know? You mean, did he confess to trashing my place and stealing my laptop? The answer to that is a big no."

He nodded, unruffled by my indignation. "Did Jeremy Rucker threaten you at all when you saw him last?"

I frowned. "No, not really. He never verbally threatened me, but he did grab my arm and tried to back me up into a tree, but…"

"But?"

"I managed to get out of his hold by striking him in the head and kicking him in the crotch."

The sheriff put his head down to write, but I saw his lips twitch a little. "And then what happened?"

"Daniel showed up and basically told Jeremy to go. Jeremy tried to hit Daniel, and Daniel punched him in the jaw, and Jeremy left."

"And this is Daniel Evans, the mayor of Frontenac City?"

"Yes."

"With whom you are having a relationship, correct?"

I glared at him. "Yes."

He didn't look at me as he wrote something else down. "After I showed up on the scene last night, what happened then? Did you return to your suite at the hotel?"

"Yes."

"With Daniel."

"Yes, he stayed over." I raised my eyebrow at him in defiance.

"And you both stayed in the suite until the morning?"

"Yes. When I woke up this morning at eight, Daniel was gone. He left me a note that he had a meeting to get to."

"Are you sure Daniel never left your suite during the night? You were pretty drunk, if I remember. Maybe you passed out, maybe—"

"Yes, I'm sure. Daniel was with me all night." Of course, he was right. I wasn't really sure when Daniel had left. But he'd made me coffee, and the coffee was hot when I got up. That was enough evidence for me.

"And you never saw Jeremy Rucker again?"

I glared at him. "Definitely not."

He nodded and then closed his notebook. "Okay, thank you for answering my questions."

I stood. "Can I leave now?"

"Yes." He stood as well, and we were nearly face to face. "I'll walk you out."

"Fine." I went to go, but turned back and grabbed the apple strudel from the table. I took a big bite of it as I passed by him and headed out the door. Damned if I was going to deny myself something delicious because of him.

Once we were out of the room, he blocked my path. "Andi, I'm sorry."

"You treated me like a suspect." I could feel tears pricking at my eyes. I wouldn't let them fall, though. Not now.

"You know I had to do it like this. I couldn't show you any favor. Considering who Jeremy is and the pending case of his, other jurisdictions could move in. This is the best way to protect you if that happens."

"We don't even know if he was killed. He could've fallen off the cliffs."

He gave me a look. "You know better than most how the gossip mill runs amok in this town."

"Fine. I understand why you did it this way. But it sucked, just so you know."

He took a step closer to me. "It sucked for me, too. You have no idea how much."

I licked my lips, suddenly aware of the narrowness of the corridor we stood in and the heat that swept over me. He reached up and drew his thumb over the side of my mouth. Apple filling covered the tip.

"You had apple on your lips."

I took in a deep breath of air. I was feeling a bit claustrophobic. "Will you let me know what the coroner says?"

"I'll see. I might have to play this close to the chest."

"Is this where you tell me not to leave town?" A smile grew across my face because of all the other times he'd said just that.

"Yes."

God, why did we have to be in the sheriff's station with a deputy standing only a few feet away? Why did we have to be in the middle of yet another possible murder investigation? Why did he have to be the sheriff? And be all noble and upstanding and so incredibly stubborn?

And so incredibly sexy it made my belly quiver.

"Sheriff?" Deputy Marshall called out. "Daniel Evans is here to see you."

The spell broke, and I took a stumbling step backward. Sheriff Jackson sighed, then took a step out of my way and allowed me to walk by. As I did, his fingers brushed against my hand. I pressed my lips together. It took everything I had not to turn back around and kiss the bastard.

When I entered the lobby, Daniel, who had been pacing, came to me and hugged me close. "Are you okay?"

"I'm good."

"Jesus, Andi. I can't believe you had to go through that. To see him like that."

I closed my eyes and inhaled his spicy scent. He really did smell amazing. "I'm fine, really."

"What did the sheriff want?" he asked as he took in my face.

"Just routine questions. Since I knew him, I could fill in some history and information."

"Okay." He drew his fingers down my face. "I guess I need to go answer some questions, too." He pressed his lips to mine softly and then kissed my forehead. "I'll call you later, okay? I have to go back to the mainland after this."

I nodded. "Okay."

He crossed the lobby and went into the back room where Sheriff Jackson waited. The moment he disappeared behind the door, I let out the breath I was holding and left the station. I had some thinking to do, and investigating, because as I'd hugged Daniel, a memory popped into my head. One where I'd woken around three a.m. and Daniel wasn't in my bed.

CHAPTER SEVEN

THE LOBBY WAS CHAOTIC when I returned to the hotel. People gathered in groups, the buzz about the body found on the rocky beach spreading from one cluster to the next, until I heard nothing but an incessant hum of words: *body, twisted, horrible, suicide...murder.*

Ginny was next to the concierge desk, helping Casey keep order. For a brief second, I felt smug satisfaction seeing the unflappable Casey actually flustered. His hands were waving, his lips yapping, and I could see the sweat on his brow.

When Ginny spotted me, she came rushing over. There were dark circles under her eyes, and she'd chewed her lipstick off. "Oh my God, it's a madhouse right now."

"I can see that."

She grabbed my hand. "How are you holding up?" She shook her head. "I can't even imagine what you are feeling right now."

"I'm okay."

She gave me a look. "How can you be?" She squeezed my hand. "Did you sleep?"

I nodded.

"Daniel stayed with you, I hope."

"Yeah, he did."

"Good. I sure wouldn't have been able to sleep alone after what happened."

I wasn't going to mention to her that I wasn't one hundred percent positive that Daniel did spend the entire night with me. He wasn't in the bed when I'd woken up in the middle of the night, but he could've been somewhere in the suite. Maybe he'd slept on the sofa, after all. Sometimes I snored when I was dead tired like that. Add that I'd been drinking, and who knew what kind of noises I'd made in my sleep.

She shook her head. "Maybe you should stay with me for a few days. I mean, first the break-in at your suite and now finding your ex-boss's body all broken and mangled…"

I frowned. The break-in. Jeremy had said I had something of his. Could he have come to the island before and searched my place? It was possible. I'd felt the sensation of being watched a time or two. I'd attributed the feeling to the deaths I'd investigated, but maybe that creepy sensation had been linked to Jeremy all along.

Ginny frowned. "What's wrong? You look like you've seen a ghost. Not surprising, considering everything."

"I've got to go back to my suite," I said. "Can you cover for me for a few hours?"

She looked out over the swarming mass of people wandering around the lobby, who were either confused about what was going on or complaining about it. She shrugged. "Sure. What the hell? Crowd control is my specialty."

She took a step forward, put her fingers into her mouth, and whistled really loud.

Every head whipped around to look at Ginny. Silence descended almost instantly. Casey turned so pale it looked like he was going to pass out. I suppressed a smile.

"Now listen up. If everyone will kindly follow me into the ballroom, we will get everything organized for the tournament tomorrow. Your itinerary is still moving forward as planned. There is nothing to be worried about."

"How about free drinks?" someone from the crowd shouted.

Ginny smiled the most winningest and flirtiest grin I'd ever seen. "Of course."

That caused a wave of cheers among the throng, and just like that, problem solved. They followed Ginny toward the grand ballroom.

I gave her a thumbs-up and headed to my suite.

The moment I was through the door, I rushed into the living room, grabbed my notebook off the table, and made a list of all the things, to the best of my knowledge, that had been in the box of personal items I was allowed to take with me when I'd been booted out of the law firm.

1. Sad little bonsai tree
2. Tiny Zen garden with sand and little rake
3. Pair of red pumps, broken right heel
4. Stack of five notebooks, all of them filled with notes
5. My "World's Okayest Lawyer" coffee mug I got as a Secret Santa gift one Christmas (still didn't know who gave it to me)
6. Hairbrush, hair clips, and elastics for a quick ponytail when I needed one

7. Cat-shaped sticky notes, also a Secret Santa gift
8. Rubber fingertip for flipping through pages of paper
9. Pretty purple Fitbit that I'd stopped using after a year
10. Pink-gold earrings which had been a gift from my parents for my thirtieth birthday
11. A framed picture of the Park family and me during my first Christmas with them
12. My favorite maroon-colored lipstick and a compact of pressed powder with a small brush
13. Pens, pencils, and markers

Now I had to think of what items I'd brought with me to the island. I might've thrown away some of that stuff, but Jeremy was adamant about his flash drive. He absolutely believed I had the damn thing. The only thing I could think of that made any sense was that he'd hidden the flash drive in something he'd thought I'd still have with me.

I set my notebook down and considered what I had thrown away. I hadn't kept the bonsai tree. It had been a sad little thing anyway, and I'd trimmed it until it was nothing but an ugly blob, so I gave up on it. I'd tossed the Zen garden as well. The little rake had broken, and I'd put it back together with green duct tape.

I went into my bedroom closet and examined my shoes. I still had the pumps. I'd fixed the heel myself, although I wasn't sure I had worn them since I left the firm. I ran my fingers over the leather. I couldn't feel any bumps or ridges. I looked at the lining. There was no place inside those pumps where a flash drive could fit. I turned the shoes over, and taking in a deep breath, I struck the heels against the edge of the table, breaking them off. I looked inside the shoes and the heels but didn't see anything. I'd ruined the pumps for no good reason.

In the bathroom, I rummaged through my makeup bag for the lipstick and the compact of pressed powder. I took the lid off the lipstick tube and twisted the lipstick up. I used this tube often, so I was sure I would've noticed something as big as a flash drive inside the tube before now. I opened my compact but couldn't see any obvious place to stash even the smallest of drives. I flipped the compact over and twisted it. It broke, and no flash drive fell out. I did similar damage to my hairbrush, breaking the handle apart. All I achieved for my sleuthing was a bunch of plastic pieces on my countertop.

My completed notebooks were in a box under the bed. I didn't like to throw them away because I never knew when I might need them. Belly on the floor, I reached under the bed and pulled the box out.

I opened the lid and went through each notebook, flipping page by page, then holding them upside down and shaking them to see if anything fell out. A ribbon bookmark with the letter A on the end and a business card for a matchmaking company in California floated to the carpet. I ran my fingers along the spines of the notebooks, but there was no way anything would fit in there, and I wasn't about to rip away the covers to confirm what I already knew.

Next, I jumped up and went into the kitchenette to find the "World's Okayest Lawyer" mug. I opened the small cupboard and found it behind two other mugs. One proclaimed the absolute universal truth that "Everything tastes better with cat hair in it," and the other one flatly stated, "I can't adult today." I took the lawyer mug out and looked it over. There was no way Jeremy could have put a flash drive in that ceramic mug. Not unless he'd broken it apart, remade it with new clay, and then fired it in a kiln.

My gaze flitted over the little teal-blue box I kept on the table as a place for all the knickknacks I didn't want lying around. Some people had junk drawers. I had a cute little junk box. The previous junk box, the one I'd used before the break-in, had been smashed to bits that night. This one was new. I'd found it in one of the shops in the village.

I walked into the living room, removed the lid, and upended the box onto the coffee table. I had a few cat-shaped sticky notes left, and I quickly flipped through the pad. Nothing stuck in there. During one of my clear-out phases, when I was sorting through the junk at the bottom of my purse, I'd tossed my old exercise tracker in the box.

I picked it up, looked at it, wondering where it could come apart. Since I hadn't used it in more than a year, I figured I wasn't about to train for a marathon anytime soon. So I smashed it onto the coffee table.

The tracker didn't break, but it cracked along the front plate. More force was required. I took it into the kitchenette, placed it on the counter. I sorted through the drawers, found a meat tenderizer tucked away, and used it like a hammer to smash the tracker with a couple of solid whacks. Little plastic pieces went everywhere. I fiddled with the front plate of the tracker and took it off. There were only electronics inside it. No flash drive.

Maybe Jeremy had been lying. Maybe he'd misplaced his flash drive and only guessed that he'd put it in my office. He would've been under a lot of pressure with the embezzlement situation hanging over his head—possibly fifteen years in prison and a mountain of debt he'd work the rest of his life to repay.

But he'd seemed so adamant about that flash drive. And he'd come all the way across the country to find it.

Jeremy was a lot of things, but he wasn't absent-minded. He absolutely believed I had possession of his flash drive. Maybe I did. I continued to search.

I opened my small jewelry box. I didn't wear a lot of jewelry. Sparkly baubles just weren't my thing. I took out the delicate gold earrings my parents had sent me from Hong Kong for my birthday. It had been one of the more thoughtful presents they'd ever given me. I flipped them over and looked at the back. Maybe if Jeremy had been a jeweler, he could've fit a tiny square flash drive into the back. But these earrings were just earrings, not holders of secret spy gadgets.

I put them back in the jewelry box and looked around my suite. I had made a mess. My gaze then landed on the framed picture of the Park family and me that I had sitting up on one of the shelves in the living room. It was the absolute last thing in the box that I'd brought with me when I moved to the island.

I took it off the shelf and carried it to the sofa. I sat down and laid the picture on the coffee table. I flipped the silver frame over and pushed up the little black hooks to remove the cardboard backing that held the photo in place. After I slipped the cardboard off, I took the photo out and placed it on the table. I picked up the boxy frame and looked it over.

My gaze homed in on the bottom right corner. The two pieces of the frame were glued together at a right angle, but they looked like they were separating a little. I got a knife from the kitchen then came back and slid the knife's tip between the two wood sides of the frame at the joint and pried them apart.

A small piece of black plastic fell out and onto the floor. I picked it up.

The black plastic square was no bigger than the tip of my finger and had tiny strips of gold metal on one side. It wasn't a bulky flash drive with a plug. It looked more like a SIM card for a cell phone.

Jeremy had hidden the thing inside the frame because he'd known I would never throw that photo away or leave it behind. He knew how important Ginny and her family were to me. I'd told him stories about Christmases and Thanksgivings I'd spent with them during my years at college.

I plopped back against the sofa cushions and stared at the tiny little card. I'd found what Jeremy had been looking for. Now I just needed to figure out how to read it.

CHAPTER EIGHT

I WENT INTO THE kitchen and found a small plastic sandwich bag. I put the tiny flash drive inside it and zipped it closed. At least now I was less likely to lose the darn thing. I was about to clean up the mess I'd made when I heard a quick knock on my door, and Ginny whirled in like a '70s-era dervish, braids swinging and a patchouli scent-cloud in her wake.

She stopped in the middle of the living room and frowned. "What is going on? Looks like another break-in."

"No, it was just me looking for something."

"What?"

"The flash drive Jeremy wanted."

"And did you find it?"

I held up the tiny plastic piece inside the sandwich bag. She leaned down and squinted at it. "It looks like a piece of plastic garbage. Where was it?"

"Stuck into the corner of my picture frame." I showed her Jeremy's hiding place.

She picked the frame up and inspected the tiny slot where the drive had been stashed. "Wow. I don't even know what to say."

"I know, right? Jeremy really wanted to hide this."

"From who?" she asked.

"No clue." I shook my head.

She set down the frame and took the drive from me, inspecting it front and back inside the baggie. "How does it go into a computer? It doesn't look like any drive I've ever used."

"It's a SIM card. It goes into a phone."

"Really? How does that work?"

I grabbed my cell phone from the table and powered it off. I looked along the side for the card slot. The slot itself was tiny and hard to find.

Once I'd located it, I plucked a paperclip from the pile of junk I'd dumped onto the coffee table. I bent the paperclip to get one end pointed out and pushed the point into the tiny hole in the slot. This caused a small plastic tray to pop out from the side of the phone.

Gently, I popped the tiny SIM card from the tray. Most of my world was embedded on that card, and I definitely didn't want to lose it. I set it carefully on the table. Then I inserted Jeremy's card into the tray and slid it into my phone. I powered the phone on.

We waited a few moments until the "enter password" screen popped up. Of course, the card was password protected. After going to so much trouble to conceal the drive, Jeremy wouldn't leave the data easily available for everyone to access.

"Bummer," Ginny said.

"Yeah." I entered a couple of number combinations. Jeremy's birthday, his daughter's birthday, his wife's birthday. Nothing worked.

"Now what do we do?" Ginny asked.

I shrugged. "Guess I have to find someone who can hack this card." I eyed my friend. "Know anyone?"

She shook her head. "Nope. I don't mingle with a techy crowd. As far as I know, I've never met an actual hacker."

I popped the tray out, removed the drive, and returned it to the baggie. Then I put my own SIM card back in my phone and checked to be sure I had everything working again.

"Where are you going to put that drive for safekeeping until you can find out what's stored on it that Jeremy thought was so damned important?"

"I'll keep it with me all the time." I retrieved my purse, took out my wallet, and slid the baggie into the place where I kept my insurance card and a variety of loyalty cards.

Ginny plopped down onto the sofa, and I started to put all the stuff on the table back into my junk box. She started helping when suddenly she put a hand on my arm to get my attention. Her eyes narrowed as she said, "Hey, do you think the break-in had something to do with this?"

"It had crossed my mind."

"You think Jeremy did it?"

"I don't know. I'm going to call a friend of mine in California who works for the courts. He'll be able to find out what Jeremy's bail conditions were. The sheriff said he wasn't allowed to leave the state. But if he flew round trip within a couple of days, no one would have known. I mean, he wasn't wearing a tracking device or anything."

"We could go to our little airport and flash his picture around, see if anyone remembers him from before," Ginny suggested.

I smiled. "That's a great idea. It's so nice to have someone to do recon with."

"We can be like Thelma and Louise." Ginny had loved that movie. She still watched it every now and then.

"Well, Thelma and Louise were running from the law and died driving off a cliff in the end," I said. "So maybe not."

"True." Ginny's enthusiasm for life was endless and perpetual. "So we can be Holmes and Watson. Or Batman and Robin."

"I'm Batman!" we both said at the exact same time, then laughed. It felt good to laugh with Ginny. It seemed like we hadn't done that often enough lately.

"Oh yeah, the reason I came…" She stood. "You're still playing in the golf tournament tomorrow, right? We need you on the team."

"Yeah, of course. I wouldn't let you down." I knocked her on the shoulder.

She grimaced. "Okay, but there's been a slight team-member change."

I sighed. "I don't like the way you're looking at me."

"Lane's going to be golfing on the team. I know you don't like him, but—"

"No, it's fine. I don't dislike him. I just think he's gunning for my job, and I'm not thrilled about that at all."

She laughed. "Yeah, he is. He even told me that one time. You'll need to be on your toes."

I shook my head but smiled. "As long as I don't have to golf with Casey, it'll be fine."

CHAPTER NINE

INSTEAD OF TAKING ONE of the hotel's golf carts to the tiny
public airport on the other side of the island, Ginny managed to
commandeer a couple of seats on one of the horse-drawn taxis
heading in that direction. She bribed the taxi driver, Rick, with
her phone number. It helped that Rick was a cutie. A bit young
for her, but definitely dateable.

The hotel's porters loaded up four departing guests and their
luggage, and we piled into the last seat. The ride was a scenic
twenty minutes through the center of the island at a leisurely
pace. Nothing happened in a hurry on Frontenac Island. We
joked that we lived in a constant state of "island time."

Rick pulled the horses up under one of the porches near the
front entrance, which looked more like a private home than a
terminal. The terminal was a white clapboard building with a
covered wrap-around porch and a copper arch over the front
entry. Back in 1934, the runway was only a strip of grass, and
the airport was used by a couple of hobbyists. Now the airport

was owned by the State Park Commission and sported an actual paved runway. During the busy seasons, the airport serviced about thirty flights a day. Two pilots took turns flying a quick hop round trip from Pellston, and the rest were private planes.

We assisted the guests off the wagon and helped to carry the luggage. Rick told Ginny he'd been called back to the village.

"Don't worry. We'll call a ride or walk back," Ginny said, waving his concerns aside.

Pellston was the closest commercial airport on the mainland. Jeremy would have changed planes twice to fly to the island, starting in California and connecting in Detroit or Chicago. Armed with a two-year-old picture of Jeremy on my phone, I followed Ginny to talk to the woman who was manning the departure gate. She beamed when she saw Ginny approach.

"Hey, Ginny! Long time no see." She hugged Ginny tight, nearly squeezing her to death, judging by the disconcerted look on Ginny's face.

"Hey, Bernadette. You're looking good."

Bernadette patted her very round backside. "I've lost twenty pounds. The Jimmy Buffet diet. Drinking lots of carrot juice and eating sunflower seeds."

"What?" I said, bewildered.

She laughed. "Just kidding. Working out, gave up beer, and watching the cheeseburgers."

"Good for you." Ginny gestured to me. "This is Andi, my friend from California. She works at the hotel now."

"Nice to meet you. Oh," her eyes lit up, "you're the one who's been running around like Nancy Drew all summer."

I balked. "Well, not exactly. I—"

She waved her hand at me. "Just kidding. I should actually thank you." She leaned in close, putting her hand close to her mouth as if to hide her words, and whispered. "I got a steal on a great house, thanks to you."

"Uh, well, you're welcome. My commission is only ten percent." I smiled.

She laughed and smacked me on the shoulder. "You're funny."

Ginny broke into the awkward conversation. "I was hoping you could help us with something."

"Sure. Anything for you."

I held up the photo of Jeremy on my phone. "Have you seen this man?"

Her eyes lit up again. "Oh yeah, I remember that tall drink of water. He was on my flight in from Pellston a few days ago."

I nodded. I had expected she'd remember his recent visit. "How about before that?"

Bernadette frowned. "Hmm, I would definitely remember him if he'd come through here before. I'm a hot-guy radar, and he only flashed on it a few days ago. Sorry."

"Anyone else who could've been working here at the time?" I asked.

"Yeah, maybe." Narrowing her eyes, her gaze swept the open terminal until she froze on a woman coming out of the restroom. She waved her hand. "Hey, Jackie!"

An older black woman waved back and smiled.

"C'mere!" Bernadette said.

Jackie hustled our way. "What's up, Bernie?" She glanced at Ginny and me with her infectious smile. She was old-fashioned and smelled like vanilla extract, which reminded me of my former nanny, Miss Charlotte. I could feel my lips twitching upward in response.

Bernadette pointed to the photo of Jeremy on my phone. "Have you seen that guy before?"

Jackie took the phone from me and really looked. She pursed her lips. "Hmm, I don't think so. He's a good-looking man, so I'd remember."

"That's what I said," Bernadette replied, hands flapping.

"Probably in and out the same day, or at most, overnight. Does that help at all?" I asked.

Jackie shook her head. "No, I'm sorry."

"Thank you anyway." Disappointment filled me. I was hoping to confirm that Jeremy had been here during the time of my break-in, because if he hadn't been the perpetrator, who was?

"You two should come by the hotel soon. It's been way too long. We'll have a few laughs, and Jackie can sing karaoke for us," Ginny said, then turned to look at me. "Jackie's got an amazing voice. Sounds like Aretha Franklin."

"I don't know about Aretha…" Jackie ducked her head modestly, but she was pleased with the praise.

"Absolutely, we'll do that," Bernadette tittered. She waved at us when we left. "Nice to have met you, Andi."

We walked out of the terminal, and I stopped and looked around. There was one hangar nearby. Maybe someone there would remember Jeremy. It was a longshot, but I didn't want to leave here without turning over every rock. This was my life fraying at the seams.

"Let's ask those guys." I pointed to a couple of workers hanging around near a couple of small private planes.

She looked at me like she knew it was a crapshoot but said, "Okay."

We asked everyone we ran into, but as I suspected, no one had seen or recognized Jeremy. Why would they? He'd have been just another tourist to them. As we left the hangar, we passed by an open door to a small office, and I caught a whiff of something familiar. I stopped and inhaled.

"What are you doing?" Ginny asked.

"Do you smell that?"

"Yeah, smells like cigarette smoke."

I nodded. "It does, but it's sweeter than American tobacco. And I've smelled it before."

Without waiting for Ginny, I walked through the open door into the small office. A large man with tattoos on his bald head was leaning back in a chair, smoking. He straightened when he saw us.

"I'm sorry, but you're not allowed in here," he said as he got to his feet and butted the cigarette into the ashtray near him.

"What are you smoking?" I asked.

He frowned. "Cigarette. I don't smoke anything else."

I put my hand up. "No, I'm sorry. I wasn't making accusations." I stepped closer to the table and the ashtray. "What kind of cigarettes are those?"

"Why?" His suspicion was raised now, and his gaze swept from me to Ginny, then back.

His evasion made me wary of him, too. So I improvised. "I remember that smell from my childhood. I'm pretty sure my grandpa smoked those. I wondered what they were."

For a moment, he eyed me defensively, and then his hand went into his overalls and pulled out a white rectangular box of cigarettes. He held them out to me. I took the box. The words on the packaging were in Cyrillic alphabet.

"Russian?"

He nodded.

"Where did you get Russian cigarettes?" I asked.

"From some guy who was around here asking questions about the planes."

"When?" My heart sped up a bit.

"He gave me a couple packs for my trouble. Honestly, I've been trying to quit."

I took out my phone and flashed a picture of Jeremy. "Is this the guy?"

He looked and then shook his head. "Nah. That wasn't him."

"What did the guy look like?"

He shrugged. "I don't know. Almost my size. Brown hair."

"Tattoos?"

He shook his head.

"Anything different about him?"

"He spoke Russian—that's all I really remember."

I nodded and snapped a quick photo of the package before I tucked my phone into my purse. "Thanks." I held up the box of cigarettes. "Can I have one?"

"Knock yourself out."

I slid one cigarette out, noticing it had a gray filter, just like the one the sheriff had recovered from the bushes near my patio. And I had smelled that sweet smoke more than once.

When we left and went back to wait for another shuttle, Ginny asked, "What was that about?"

I held up the cigarette. "I'm pretty sure whoever gave that guy these smokes is the same person who broke into my suite."

Ginny looked toward the terminal. Another horse-drawn taxi had moved in to drop off a passenger. "Come on, let's catch that taxi while we can."

We hoofed it over to the entrance and hopped up into the empty carriage.

CHAPTER TEN

ʼOH MY GOD, ANDI, are you sure?" Ginny asked as the horses pulled the taxi toward the village.

"I can't be one hundred percent sure, but I'd put a hefty wager on it."

"What are you going to do?"

"Talk to the sheriff about it."

"Where can we drop you two?" the taxi driver asked.

"The sheriff's station, please," I replied. We plodded along into the village and stopped in front of the station just as Ginny's cell phone buzzed with a text. She checked it, then texted back with speedy thumbs.

"Lois needs me at the hotel. There's some urgent matter."

"I'll walk back," I said.

"Are you sure?"

"Yup." I opened the door and jumped out. "I'll see you later."

Once the taxi carried Ginny away, I went into the station hoping to find the pleasant Deputy Marshall behind the counter.

I was sorely disappointed when Deputy Shawn gave me a wide saccharine smile.

"Well, hello there, Nancy Drew. How may I help you?"

"Hey, Barney Fife," I replied with annoyance, and he scowled at me. I hadn't seen him in a while and had hoped the sheriff had made good on his promise to transfer Shawn out. No such luck. "Is Sheriff Jackson in his office?"

"Nope. The sheriff is out and about."

"Do you know where he is?"

"Nope."

I shook my head. Of course he didn't. And even if he'd known, he wouldn't have told me. Deputy Shawn liked me about as much as I liked him. Which was to say, not much.

"Have a nice day," he called after me in a singsong voice when I left.

Since I had to pass the shop on my way up Market Street to the hotel, I decided to pop into June's Blooms to check on her. She would probably think I was there to see when she was leaving the island so I could move into her house. That wasn't the *only* reason I was popping in. I truly wanted to see if she was okay. She'd gone through hell recently.

I pushed the door to the flower shop open, the little bell overhead dinging, and the two birds in the cage by the door announced my arrival as they usually did.

"Customer!" they both screamed.

I turned to the counter as someone came out from the back, but it wasn't June like I'd expected.

"Sasha?"

She smiled at me as she swept at the dark curls that dropped onto her forehead. "Hey."

"What are you doing here?"

June stepped out from the back room. "I'm training her as a customer service rep for when I go on my vacation."

"I didn't know you knew anything about flowers," I said to the girl. The last time I'd seen her was when I'd saved her from a ranting maniac. Before that, I'd unexpectedly helped deliver her baby boy.

"I took some online courses, and when I moved back to the island, I ran into June, and she mentioned needing some help at the shop."

"Wow. That's…that's great. How's…I'm sorry, but I don't think you ever told me your son's name."

"Liam."

"That's a great name. How is he?"

"Growing up. You'd probably not even recognize him."

I probably wouldn't. I figured babies all looked the same until they were toddlers.

"Can I talk to you?" I motioned for June to come outside with me. "It was great to see you again, Sasha. I'm glad you're doing so well."

Once outside, I whirled on June. "Are you sure she's a good choice to work the shop while you're gone?"

"She's qualified and personable."

"She was involved with a murder case."

June pressed her lips into a tight line. "So was I."

"That was different."

"How? She got involved with the wrong man. So did I, apparently." She shrugged. "I have a soft spot for wayward women."

She dropped her gaze.

"Okay, but she's not taking care of the business, right?"

She gave me a look. "Of course not. Actually, Nicole Park is going to take over running the business for me."

"Nicole?"

She nodded. "I guess you didn't know that she's leaving the Park Hotel."

I didn't know, and I was guessing neither did most of the Park family. Ginny hadn't said a word about it. I hoped the hotel was all she was leaving. I knew she and Eric had been having marital problems. At one point, Nicole would've accused me of being one of those problems. I wondered if this was the urgent matter Ginny needed to address when she'd received that text from Lois.

"Okay, well, I'll check in with you later," I said.

"Just so you know, I'm planning on leaving soon. So you'll have some time to get your things moved into the house before the snow falls."

I smiled and gave her a hug. Then I hurried up to the hotel.

Chapter Eleven

WHEN I GOT BACK, instead of going into the lobby, I went around the hotel to the other side where the family suites were located. I wanted to get a different view of my suite from the path that wound through the grounds and along the west bluff.

I crossed the grass and approached my patio. I stood near the bushes on the left side of the cement partition, where the sheriff had found the cigarette butt. I looked down at the ground to see if there were any more. I hadn't expected to find any because the lawn maintenance staff at the Park, like everything else, was top-notch. Everyone who worked there made sure the place was as sparkling clean as humanly possible.

I stood there, envisioning myself as a man lying in wait, watching me, waiting for an opportunity. I surveyed the grounds. From this spot, I could see most of everything going on around me, but I didn't think too many people could see me. It was a good hiding spot. Which probably meant no one had noticed him standing there. Heck, a lot of the guests at that time, who might have seen something unusual, were long gone.

My gaze landed on a spot near the west bluff less than a hundred yards away from my suite. I could see a couple of people standing near the edge, police tape flapping in the wind. I immediately recognized Sheriff Jackson. He turned and watched me as I trekked across the manicured lawn toward him.

"Hey," he said.

I crept closer to the edge and peered over to see the rocky beach below. This must've been where Jeremy had...what? Jumped? Fallen? Been pushed? A shiver racked my body, and I felt the sheriff's hand on my arm, helping me take a few steps back.

"Find anything helpful here?" I asked.

"Nothing definitive. Lots of foot traffic in this area. Hard to distinguish tracks and footprints."

"Do you think he fell or was pushed?"

"Because of where he was found, I'm fairly certain he was pushed. If he'd simply fallen, his body would've landed closer to the bluff."

Trying to wrap my head around it, I repeated, "So he was pushed."

"Looks like it," the sheriff replied quietly.

I nodded. I'd been hoping that he'd simply fallen. That it somehow had been a terrible accident. Like he'd stumbled or lost his footing or something like that. Now, it looked like he'd been murdered.

I reached into my purse and pulled out the cigarette the guy at the airport had given me. I handed it to the sheriff. Frowning, he took it.

"Um, I don't smoke."

"This is the same type of cigarette you found outside my place. It's Russian."

"What?"

I told him about our trip to the airport and what the guy with the tattooed head had told me.

"Why would some Russian man break into your suite?"

I shrugged. "I don't know, but maybe it had something to do with Jeremy."

He sighed and shook his head. "I don't like this, Andi. There is something so very wrong about all of this."

"I know."

We stopped talking when an elderly woman walking with a cane approached us. "Good afternoon," she said.

Sheriff Jackson tipped his hat. "Ma'am."

"Good afternoon," I said to her.

"Are you investigating the garbage dumpers?"

I frowned, as did the sheriff. "Pardon?" he said.

"I was wondering if you were here about the people who dumped all that garbage over the bluff. I hate polluters, don't you?" She looked at me.

"I do. Absolutely. Are you a guest at the hotel?" I asked.

She nodded. "Yes, I am. Lovely hotel, lovely place. That's why it's so despicable when someone litters." She shook her head. "I mean, why dump a big bag of clothes like that? They could be donated, at the very least. Such a waste."

"You saw someone dump a bag of clothes over the bluff?" the sheriff asked.

She nodded. "Oh yes, the other night."

"What time was this?" He took out his notebook.

"Late. Sometimes I can't sleep—the arthritis acts up." She touched her leg. "So I like to walk. I came out here. It was dark, but I'm not scared." She lifted her cane. "I'd knock some sense into anyone who tried anything with me."

I smiled at her. "Of course you would. Me, too."

"I was walking along this path, and I saw someone drag a big bag of clothes and then toss it over onto the beach."

"Was this someone a man or a woman?" Sheriff Jackson asked.

"Oh, I'm sure it was a man. He was too tall for a woman."

"Did you see what he looked like?"

She shook her head. "It was dark, and I didn't have my glasses on."

He gave her a tight smile but continued. "Where were you when you saw this man?"

She pointed down the path with her cane. "I was walking from that way. I stopped at that bench and sat for a spell. And that's when I saw him."

I looked at the bench she pointed to. It had to have been thirty yards from the bluff. Without her glasses, she could only have seen vague, dark shapes. What she assumed she'd seen was a man dragging a big bag of clothes. But what she could've seen was a man dragging Jeremy's body to the edge and pushing it off.

The sheriff nodded to her. "Well, thank you for sharing this. Would it be possible to get your name and a way to get in touch with you for our records?"

"Oh yes, certainly. I'm always happy to help out the police. It's important to be an active member of society. I've seen too many times when people don't do anything."

"Me, too," he said.

"My name is Carol Jacobs." She rattled off her cell phone number, and he wrote it down.

"Oh, you're from Ontario," the sheriff said.

"I am. Sudbury. But every few years, I try to come to Frontenac Island. It's such a beautiful place. Don't you think, dear?" She looked at me.

"I do." I smiled at her. "You know, I work here at the hotel." I gave her one of my business cards.

"Oh, that's nice."

"I'd like to offer you a free breakfast tomorrow morning, for being so helpful."

"That is so sweet of you. Thank you."

"What room are you in? I'll make sure to let the restaurant know."

"I'm in 234."

The sheriff tipped his hat to her again. "You've been very helpful, Mrs. Jacobs."

"Just doing my duty." She gave us a nod and then started to go about her way, but she suddenly stopped and turned back around. "Oh, Miss Steele, you should probably have a talk with your staff about what happened."

"Why's that?"

"Because I assume he either works at your hotel or is a guest." The sheriff and I glanced at each other, both of us frowning.

"What makes you say that, Mrs. Jacobs?" the sheriff asked.

"Because after dumping the clothes, he ran back to the hotel."

We both stepped closer to her. "Did you see where he went exactly?"

She nodded and lifted her cane to point. "There. He ran toward that room. The one with the azalea bushes."

I followed the visual direction, my stomach churning and my mouth going dry. She was pointing toward my suite.

Chapter Twelve

AFTER WE THANKED MRS. Jacobs for her help, Sheriff Jackson and I walked to my suite. I had to take extra strides to keep up with his brisk pace. I could almost see the wheels turning in his head.

Breathlessly, I said, "Come on, Luke. There's no way Daniel left my suite, found Jeremy, had a fight with him, then threw him off the bluff."

He stopped dead in his tracks and stared at me. "That was *not* what I was thinking."

"Oh." I looked around sheepishly.

"Why are you worried about that? Did something happen?"

"I'm not worried."

"You are, or it wouldn't have popped into your head."

I wondered if I should tell him that when I woke up around 3 a.m., Daniel wasn't in bed with me. I couldn't be sure he wasn't in my suite somewhere, so I'd decided to keep that information to myself. There could've been a million different reasons why he wasn't in bed. And one of them was definitely not to go out and murder a man who had threatened me and basically ruined my life. Daniel simply wasn't that kind of guy.

I replied, "Nothing happened. I'm not worried that Daniel killed Jeremy. Because he didn't. Simple as that."

The sheriff eyed me for another long moment. "You would tell me, though…if something happened to make you suspicious of Daniel?"

Before I could respond, he broke his gaze and turned toward the patio of my suite. "According to Mrs. Jacobs, the man came here. Why? Was he planning to break in?"

"How would I know?" I replied.

Frowning, he looked at me. "Did you leave your balcony blinds open?"

"Probably. I don't often shut them."

He shook his head. "That's just irresponsible, Andi. You're a pretty young woman living alone. You should take more care."

I made a face. "Are you blaming me?"

"No." His frown deepened. "That's not what I'm doing. I'm just saying it's like leaving your door unlocked and wide open—"

"Oh my God, you *are* blaming me." I felt my face flush and my heartbeat quicken, not in a good way.

Sheriff Jackson raised his hand, palm out. "I'm not blaming you. Get that out of your head. I'm just saying that maybe he saw Daniel inside your place and decided to not come in."

Then I had an epiphany. "So, you think the same guy who broke into my suite could be the same guy who threw Jeremy off the bluff?"

He rubbed his chin. "There's nothing actually tying the two events together."

"But it's possible."

"That theory is complete speculation at this point, Andi. Nothing more." He sighed and rubbed his chin again. "I do think that you need to be more careful. You are definitely connected to this case. You knew the victim, and he claimed that you had something of his in your possession, which he wanted badly enough to risk violating his parole and going to prison for. He was killed for a reason, and you seem to be involved, whether you want to be or not."

I thought about the tiny card in my wallet. I probably should've handed it over to the sheriff, but I needed to know what was on it first. The contents could be the reason why Jeremy was killed. They could also be the reason I'd lost everything that was important to me, and I didn't want to give that over to someone else.

Not yet. Not until I knew exactly what I'd be handing over.

"I'll be more careful," I said finally.

Sternly, as if he were talking to his daughter or something, he said, "That means no running off looking for evidence, either."

I looked at him for a second longer than was probably polite. "I said I'll be more careful."

"Andi…" he said with a long, exasperated sigh.

"Luke…" I mimicked him.

"You are impossible." He shook his head and turned to walk away. I followed him. I needed him for…to…I maybe just needed him.

I caught up and grabbed his arm. "Okay. You win. How about if I feel like I'm going to go running off after evidence that might be dangerous in some way, I'll call you first? Fair?"

"This is not a game. You could get seriously hurt. You're involved somehow." He ran a hand through his hair. "Don't you get that? Whoever killed Jeremy Rucker is playing for keeps."

I put my hand up toward him. "I swear I didn't kill Jeremy and toss him off the cliff like a duffel bag of old clothes."

He shook his head again, but this time, there was a ghost of a smile on his lips. I was getting better at this. He wasn't staying mad at me for long anymore. Annoyed most likely, frustrated most definitely, but not angry. That was indeed progress.

"I know, but whoever did kill him is circling around you in some way and for some reason. That much is fact." His cell phone buzzed from his pocket. He took it out and answered it.

"Jackson." He nodded, grunted, then said, "I'll be right over." He returned his phone to his pocket. "The autopsy report is finished."

My eyes lit up.

"No, you can't come with me."

"Will you call me later and let me know?" I cocked an eyebrow. "You're the one who says this is connected to me, so surely I should have all pertinent information, including how Jeremy died."

He frowned and stared at me again. "You make all of this really hard, you know."

"What, your job?"

"No. The other part." Then he walked away, and I stood there watching him go, dumbfounded. What did he mean "the other part"? What was the other part?

Still contemplating what the sheriff had said, I went into the hotel to check on the Park family. I wanted to find Ginny and see if Nicole's decision to leave the hotel was the emergency Lois had texted her about.

As I crossed the lobby, I heard raised voices at the concierge desk, which was never a good sign. Casey was arguing with a clearly upset young woman, whom I recognized as Melanie, the assistant of the jerk I'd dealt with the other morning.

"I'm sorry," Casey was saying, "but we can't cover your drinks for the whole weekend."

Melanie was close to tears. "But the other concierge told me to charge my bill to my room and she would take care of it."

Casey folded his arms across his chest. "Well, she doesn't have the authority to make decisions like that. I'm the chief concierge, and Ms. Steele is a junior staff member. You're going to have to pay for those drinks."

I approached the desk. "Hi, Melanie. Good to see you again. Is everything okay?"

Casey flinched, apparently not expecting me—and not ready to take me on, either. Smart man.

Melanie shook her head, showing me the sheet with her room charges on it. "He's telling me that I'm going to have to pay for these charges. I really can't afford to pay this bill."

I took the invoice from her. "Don't worry. I'll make sure these charges don't go on your credit card."

Casey sputtered, "You can't—"

I cut him off with a look.

"Really?" Melanie said with a tremulous smile.

"Yes, I promised you free food and drinks, and you shall have them. It's a fair trade, I think, for having to put up with a really horrid boss for the weekend." I smiled at her, then turned and looked at Casey with the same grin. Casey wasn't my boss, whether he wanted to think so or not.

"Thank you." She visibly sagged against the counter. "It's Andi, right?"

"It certainly is, and don't hesitate to give me a call if you have any more problems." I handed her one of my business cards. "The Park Hotel appreciates every valued guest."

She gave me a big smile. "I'll never forget this." Then she walked off.

Casey huffed. "You can't just give free stuff to people willy-nilly. Everything comes out of the profits of the hotel."

"Don't you think customer service is more important?"

"Not always."

I gave him a withering look. "That woman is an assistant to a very important CEO of a huge company. I guarantee you she is the one who books events, and she's the one who decides where such events will take place and where the CEO and staff stay at such events. She is also the one who books his family holidays. He also loves to golf. So, where is she likely to suggest for his family holiday next year? Or maybe even the next company retreat?"

Casey rolled his eyes. "You don't know any of that."

"You're right, I don't. Not for sure. But it's way more likely than not. What do you think the result would have been if I'd let you force her to pay?" His eyes bugged out of his head. I glanced over his shoulder and then smiled sweetly. "We can ask Samuel, if you'd prefer."

He opened his mouth, and I expected a slew of bad language to be coming out of it, but Samuel appeared at the desk, and Casey quickly snapped his mouth shut. It literally made a snapping sound.

"Hello, Samuel," I said with a smile.

"Andi." He nodded.

"Good afternoon, Samuel." Casey preened. "I was just trying to explain some of the finer points of being a concierge, things I think she's failing to grasp."

"Oh, really?" Samuel said. "I think Andi has a fine grasp on all aspects of being a concierge."

Casey pursed his lips.

Samuel took my arm. "I hear you're going to be golfing on the Park Hotel team tomorrow."

"Yes, I'm very excited to represent the hotel." I gave Casey a side-eye look. "You know who's also on the team? Lane, from the front desk. He's a wonderful asset to the team and to the hotel."

"Is that right?" We walked together, arm in arm, away from the concierge desk.

"Yes, he's usually my go-to guy when I need someone to cover the desk. I think he'd make a great concierge one day." I glanced over my shoulder at Casey to make sure he heard every word.

The eye daggers he shot me could have been lethal. But the exchange made me smile, anyway.

Once we were across the lobby and out of earshot, Samuel stopped and gestured to one of the green sofas near the big bay window. We sat. I was nervous because I'd never taken a pause with Samuel before. He was usually always on the go and not interested in spending any extra time with me.

"I heard what you said about the hotel," he said.

"Sorry about that. Casey just—"

"I know…he can be irritating." He shook his head and gave a wistful smile. "You wouldn't believe some of the stuff we'd do way back when I worked in the hotels in Chicago. The concierges at competing hotels would actually sabotage each other." He laughed. "Oh, some of the hijinks I could tell you."

I watched his expression change from wistful to worried. Something was bothering him. "Are you concerned about Nicole leaving the hotel? Are she and Eric…?"

He glanced at me. "Oh, you heard about that?"

I nodded. "June told me."

"No, I'm not worried. Eric and Nicole will be fine. All marriages have ups and downs. It's how they weather the downs that matters most."

"What's going on, then? You look worried about something."

"Have you seen or heard Lois talking to herself?" He looked down at the floor while he asked.

I wanted to say no, but Samuel asked out of real concern for his daughter-in-law, whom I knew he loved very much. "Yes, a couple of times."

"She thinks she's talking to Henry." He sighed. "Which would be okay if that's all it was. I talked to Loraine for years after she passed. But Lois thinks he's still here. She is hearing Henry talking back to her. That's not healthy."

"Have you talked to her about it?"

He shook his head. "Henry's sudden death was so hard on her—on all the family, really. It was a blow I'm not sure she's recovered from."

"Lois is tough. She's the strongest woman I know. You're not worried about how she's running the hotel, are you?" Whatever happened, Lois ran the Park Hotel with a firm and steady hand. She was good at her job, and she loved the Park.

"No. She's making good decisions. I just worry."

"Of course you do. Any good father would."

He turned his head toward me and patted my hand. "You're a good woman, Andi. You're good for this hotel and good for my family. I hope we never lose you." He stood and, after fixing his tie, wandered back across the lobby, doing his rounds.

I sat back in the sofa for a moment, soaking up the compliment Samuel had given me. He'd taken me by surprise. I'd never had a close family. Growing up had been lonely. My parents weren't close to their siblings, so there were no big family gatherings on holidays. I never had big birthday celebrations with lots of presents and family and friends. If it hadn't been for Miss Charlotte, I would've been a very isolated child.

The Parks were a huge blessing that came into my life when I met Ginny. I never wanted to take any of that for granted.

I glanced up at the clock and realized that I was late for my meeting with the hunky and mysterious Clive Barrington. I rushed to my suite to get ready.

Barrington had reminded me several times of my promise to join him for dinner. I had hoped he would finish his business on the island, whatever it was, and leave long before this day arrived. No such luck. Something about him made me uneasy, so I'd been avoiding him and hoping he'd get the hint. No such luck. I also tried setting him up with Ginny a couple of times. I could tell that she liked him and had a good time with him, which made us both happy. But Mr. Gorgeous, as Ginny had been calling him, was still here, and he had asked me about dinner again three days ago—in a way that suggested he'd never give up and I might as well give in. So, I sucked it up and agreed.

I had made the reservation for a time when I was sure Ginny wouldn't be available to join us. I would normally have invited her to come along, but I wanted to have a private chat with the mysterious stranger and get it over with. This was my chance.

Chapter Thirteen

WE'D MET IN THE lobby of the Park and strolled down to the
village, and now we were seated at Top of the Lilac, perched atop
the fourth floor of the Lilac Inn on Main Street. From here, we had
a stellar view of the Round Island lighthouse and the impressive
Mighty Mac bridge connecting Michigan's upper and lower
peninsulas. I also had a spectacular view of Barrington. He was just
as hunky and charming as Ginny had said. He might be perfect for
her, but he was a little too perfect for me. I never wanted to date a
guy who was better looking than I was. Too much pressure.

By the time we'd arrived at our table, I'd exhausted all of my
usual small talk about the island's most popular features. He had
listened intently and asked insightful questions. I had the
impression that he was genuinely interested in every word,
which unnerved me a little. I'm a fairly good conversationalist,
but in all my life, I had never inspired any man to give me his
undivided attention. Certainly not a man as awesome as Clive
Barrington. I'm just not that fascinating.

Call me skeptical if you want, but the whole situation made me suspicious.

After we'd ordered our meal, and an expensive bottle of red wine to go with it, Barrington remained as relaxed and at ease as ever. I, on the other hand, felt like a tightly coiled spring. I took another sip of wine to loosen me up a bit.

"Tell me, Ms. Steele," he began in that sexy, rumbly voice with charm for days, "how did you end up working as the concierge at the Park Hotel? Didn't Lane tell me you're a lawyer?"

The question was troubling. There was nothing on my business card that said I had been a damn good lawyer once upon a time. He had been asking around about me, and I didn't like it. Not even a little bit. Who else had he been asking? And what did they tell him? Perhaps I should have been flattered, but his interest only made me more uneasy. Our comfortable, very public environment emboldened me, though. Or maybe it was the wine. Either way, I was inspired by the little devil sitting on my shoulder to cut right to the chase and find out what was going on.

"The Park is a beautiful and special place, isn't it?" I sidestepped his question adroitly and then gave him a nice smile and slid over to my own inquisition. "What kind of business brings you here all the way from Hong Kong?"

"I wondered how long it would take you to ask me that." He flashed me one of his megawatters like I was a star pupil or something.

I returned his smile and bit my tongue, resisting the temptation to rush in and fill the awkward silence which lasted until after the waiter delivered our salads. He fell on his food like a hungry wolf while I waited, my salad untouched. When my stomach began to growl loudly enough to be heard all the way over in Frontenac City, I gave in and took a bite.

He finally replied, looking at me directly through those amazing green eyes. The kind of look that would make a girl's toes tingle. "I'm a fixer for your parents at Club Paradise."

His words caused me to choke on the salad, and I spent the next few seconds trying to swallow instead of spitting my romaine all over the table. I washed the last of it down with a big gulp of water while he grinned at my discomfort.

"I gather that's not what you expected me to say? You have so many visitors to Frontenac Island from Hong Kong, do you? The connection simply didn't occur to you, Andi? I'm sure you're more clever than that. Surely you already knew that your parents sent me here," he said calmly. Giving me a chance to regain my composure, he sipped his wine and took a moment to appreciate the smooth finish. "I'm very impressed with the quality of the wines available here. This little island is more upscale than I expected. It's obvious why you like the place."

I sat back in my chair and folded my hands over my napkin. "Mr. Barrington—"

"Please call me Clive. Your parents, Drew and Emily, are good friends. I'm sure you and I will be, too."

Every word out of his mouth made me nervous. I had assumed there was some connection between Barrington's arrival on Frontenac Island and my parents, sure. But I had been ignoring the internal warnings from my queasy stomach every time he made excuses to talk to me. "Okay, Clive. Are you saying my parents sent you here? For what purpose?"

"To offer you a job. What did you think? Were you worried that I might kidnap you and haul you back to Hong Kong against your will?" He cocked his head and smiled.

"Not at all," I replied, although I actually had been thinking along those lines. Now that he'd said the words aloud, the idea didn't seem foolish. I'd experienced a little too much drama, and I allowed my imagination to run amok.

The waiter collected the salad plates—Clive's as clean as if it had come directly from the dishwasher, and mine barely touched. He refilled our wineglasses and discreetly departed. During the process, I had a few minutes to think.

"I'm sorry your trip has been wasted. I've already told my parents that I'm not interested in moving to Hong Kong. I've told them that many, many times over the years. My life is here. I like living in this country, Clive. In fact, I like living on this island. I love the Park Hotel, and I really love my job. Apparently, they still haven't accepted my decision. I'm sorry to have wasted your time, but I'm not sure what more I can do." I sipped my wine and pretended to relax.

Now that I knew why he was here, he seemed less threatening. Maybe I could still set him up with Ginny. She had made it clear she'd be thrilled to spend time with him.

Barrington nodded in a friendly way and leaned forward. Quietly, he said, "Forgive me, Andrea, but your decision makes no sense."

I gasped at his impertinence. He knew almost nothing about me. This was the longest conversation we'd ever had. Surely, whomever he had been asking must have told him that making logical, rational decisions was one of the things I did best. The only thing I could think of to say in response was, "Why not?"

"Your life is at a crossroads. You aren't practicing law here, and it's not likely you ever will, based on the embezzlement files I've read. You're single, and there is nothing holding you here. You don't own a home, don't have a real job. You don't have children or a spouse tying you down. The only things tying you to this place are your beloved cats, and they don't even live with you now." He paused for another sip of wine and to give a chance for his logic to overwhelm me. "As charming as Frontenac Island is, nothing here can compare to Hong Kong. And of course, you can bring Scout and Jem with you. No problem at all."

I could feel my cheeks flush and my ears warming. The longer he talked, the more annoyed I became. His argument was so persuasively laid out that I even found myself nodding along involuntarily.

"Club Paradise is presenting you with a phenomenal opportunity anyone would die for, and you're throwing it away with both hands. Your parents simply don't understand why, and neither do I." He paused again and gave me a penetrating gaze. "This job won't wait forever, Andi. Your parents aren't getting any younger. Club Paradise is a wonderful business. It should be yours one day. Do you really want to give all of that up?"

I tried to find something to say to prove him wrong on one single point, but facts were facts, and he had not misstated any. The way he'd laid it all out, only an idiot would make the choices I had made. Problem was, I kind of agreed with him. Was I just being a petulant child after all?

The waiter returned with our meals and placed the plates in front of us. Again, Clive ate his meal with gusto while I pushed the food around on my plate with a fork. A bright orange sunset lit the western sky over Lake Michigan, bathing everything on the island in a warm glow.

I gazed at the sunset and thought about all the things I loved about my new home, the Park family, Daniel, all my new friends. Even the sheriff. Could I leave it all behind and move around the world? What about Ginny?

He finished his meal, and we left, walking back the way we'd come. As we approached the Park, he said, "I'll be here a few more days, and then I will need to get back. I can talk to you about the job, answer any questions you might have. If I return to Hong Kong without you, Drew and Emily will need to hire another candidate. I'm sure you understand."

Involuntarily, I gasped, and my eyes widened. "My parents are planning to sell Club Paradise?"

"That's what they sent me here to make clear, Andi. To find out for sure whether you truly don't want the business. They've received offers over the years and always rejected them, but this one is compelling. And it has an expiration date. Unless you want to take your rightful ownership role in Club Paradise, they'll have no other choice." He opened the big front door with a flourish. I walked inside, and he followed. "Look around, Andi. The Park Hotel is a grand place, filled with history and sentiment. Yet, Club Paradise is ten times more grand than the Park. Like the Parks, your parents have spent their lives building the business for their only child. Would Ginny and Eric turn their backs on the Park the way you're doing with Club Paradise?"

He thanked me for a lovely evening, tipped his head in that continental way that gave him a gentlemanly air, and headed for the elevators. He'd left me with much to consider.

CHAPTER FOURTEEN

THE GOLF TOURNAMENT STARTED at six o'clock the next morning. I was in group five, out of eight total, and we didn't tee off until seven o'clock. I'd slept fitfully. Between bouts of extreme panic that I hadn't locked the door or the balcony and getting up to check, I lay awake staring at the ceiling, trying to figure out who broke into my suite and why and how the break-in was connected to Jeremy.

When I'd tired of worrying about all of that, I'd lie on my side, staring at my phone, wondering if Sheriff Jackson was interested in me, as his daughter had implied. Was that what he'd meant by "the other part"? Was he saying he had feelings for me?

When I showed up at the clubhouse with the largest mug of black coffee and looking a little rough despite my well-put-together outfit, I wasn't surprised by Lane's once-over.

"Do you want to use my hemorrhoid cream?" he asked.

I made a face. "Excuse me?"

"For the bags under your eyes. It works wonders. Shrinks the swelling down in seconds."

I quickly searched for a reflective surface to study my face. Sure enough, he was right. My eyes came packing with a whole set of luggage. I held out my hand, and he placed a small tube of Preparation H into it.

I excused myself to go to the ladies' room. At the mirror, I dabbed the ointment liberally around my eyes. In seconds, my bags disappeared. I returned to join our team and discreetly handed the tube back to Lane.

"Thanks."

"No problem."

The rest of our foursome arrived: Eric Park and Justin Hamilton, our world-class chef at the restaurant. He was also the mayor's husband and an extremely affable man. I hoped he was a good golfer. Not that we were in it to win it. Sure, I was more than a tad competitive. But I wanted desperately to beat Mr. Fasco's team. The prizes went to charity, so it didn't *really* matter.

"Morning," I said to them both.

"Morning, Andi," Justin said.

Eric simply nodded. He looked like he hadn't slept well, either. I hoped I'd get a chance to talk to him during the day. We'd been good friends years ago when Ginny and I were in college. We'd not been that close since, but I enjoyed talking with him. Since moving to the island, I could probably count on one hand how many conversations we'd actually had.

"Are we ready?" Eric asked us.

We took our bags out to our cart, and with Eric driving, we wheeled up to the tee. Another team was already there setting up their shots. I recognized Mr. Minsky from the ferry.

He saw me and smiled. "Beautiful day for golf, don't you think, Ms. Steele?" he said.

"Couldn't agree more."

Lane snickered. "He's totally flirting with you."

"No, he isn't. He's just being friendly." I pulled my golf glove on. It was sparkly gold, to match the golf bag I'd borrowed. I pulled my driver out. "Besides that, he is totally not my type."

"Yeah, you go for the tall, dark, and handsome type," Lane said. "If they're authority figures, you like them even better."

I was about to argue with him, but the truth was, he was right.

"Yeah, Andi does certainly have a type." This from Eric.

I frowned at him. "I don't have a type."

"Remember that guy you went out with in college?" he said. "Ian something? He was tall, dark hair, and wasn't he an associate professor?"

"Adjunct professor at the law school, actually. He was a public defender. He didn't teach full time."

"Still, he had authority at the college, and you gravitate that way, like Lane said." Eric pulled his driver and a bright yellow ball from his bag, preparing to tee off.

I detected a thread of resentment in his voice but shook it off. Dating Ian had been a mistake. He wasn't the man I'd initially thought he was. He didn't have a healthy respect for the law or for his clients. I'd observed how he'd treated a poor young Hispanic man who needed help, and that was enough for me to know the measure of his character. I stopped dating him that very moment.

I remembered telling Eric about it, and shortly after that was when Eric had asked me out. I knew within the first hour that it wouldn't work between us. At least not for me. Ginny had told me that Eric had felt differently. Which was why Nicole hadn't been friendly to me when I first arrived on the island. She believed Eric was still in love with me. I didn't think that at all, but there were some awkward moments since I'd come to the Park that had given me pause. I really hoped their marital issues had nothing to do with me.

After Eric drove his ball an impressive 200 yards, I teed up next. I set my pink ball on the tee, lined up, and swung. The ball sailed through the air. There was nothing like smacking a golf ball and seeing it fly. It landed beyond Eric's.

While Justin set up and Lane prepared to go next, I went to stand beside Eric.

"I heard about Nicole leaving the hotel to work at June's. Is everything else okay with the two of you?"

"I know you like to be in everyone's business, Andi, but please stay out of mine." He walked away from me and jumped into his cart.

I frowned after him. Was that how he really saw me? A nosy busybody?

After Lane finished his tee shot, I took the passenger's seat in Lane's cart, and we drove down to our balls. Poor Justin had sliced to the right. He wasn't quite into the trees but was close enough.

"You wouldn't consider me a busybody, would you?" I asked Lane.

He shook his head. "No, not really. I think you honestly like helping people."

I rewarded him with a smile. "Thank you for noticing."

"Yeah, like I heard what you said to Mr. Park today. About me being a good concierge."

"I said you *might* be a good one in the future."

"Same thing. I thought it was really nice."

He didn't have to know I had ulterior motives for saying it. I'd wanted to irritate Casey, and I had succeeded gloriously.

We all played the hole fairly well. I'd sunk my putt one under, Eric and Lane shot par, and Justin hit one over for the hole. At the next hole, Eric drove his ball at least 220 yards. He landed on the green and very close to the flag. I went next and hit a respectable drive straight down the fairway.

When we were all back in our carts, Lane took out his phone. He used his fingerprint to open it and utilized an app to calculate his next shot and determine what club he needed. It was all very impressive. As I watched him, I thought about Jeremy's flash drive hiding in my wallet and how I might find out how to read it.

"Hey," I said, "you look like you're pretty techy."

"Yeah, I like my gadgets," Lane replied.

I kept my voice low. "Would you know how to open up an encrypted SIM card?"

He glanced at me. "Hmm, very intriguing. Whose card?"

"I can't tell you that."

He grinned. "Oh, now I'm totally interested."

"Can you help me?" I asked.

"Yes, but..."

"But what?"

"You have to help me with Mr. Park."

I smiled. "Technically, I already have."

"I want to be a concierge," Lane said.

"Well, you can't have my job."

He nodded. "I know. I want Casey's."

The carts stopped, and we stepped out. "I can't promise you Casey's job, but I can help to nudge him out for you."

"Deal." He held out his hand, and we shook on it.

While Lane chipped his ball onto the green, I went to grab my six iron from my bag, but the club wasn't there. I took out the seven iron instead and hit my ball a foot from the hole. We putted in and moved on.

We played the third hole without a hitch. On the fourth hole, Justin sliced again and ended up in the sand trap on the right side of the green. After I sunk my ball, I walked over to keep him company and cheer him on. It seemed like he was off his game. What I liked about him, though, was he never lost his good nature.

"I don't know what's wrong with me today," he said as he slid the pitching wedge from his bag.

"Hey, we all have off days," I said. "If we didn't, we'd all be Tiger Woods."

He chuckled. "I just can't seem to concentrate. Too much on my plate, I guess."

I laughed at his pun.

"I guess my plate will overflow when the baby comes." He took a practice swing above the sand.

"What? You and Lindsey are going to have a baby?"

He nodded, chuckling. "Yeah, we haven't told anyone yet. Actually, Lindsey will probably kill me that I told you."

"I can totally keep a secret." I went over to him and offered my hand. "Congratulations. That's great news."

"Thanks. We're really excited, but with reelection coming up next year, Lindsey is a bit nervous."

"Hey, everyone loves a pregnant lady. She'll be a shoo-in."

Justin lined up his shot, swung his club…and missed the ball. He laughed and shook his head. "I think I have more pregnancy-brain than Lindsey does." He lined up again and swung. This time, he hit the ball out of the sand trap, but we heard a metal clinking sound.

"I think I hit something else besides the ball." He frowned down at the sand trap.

I joined him, and we looked into the trap. I couldn't see anything sticking out. We used our clubs and combed through the sand. Together we dug around until I hit something unyielding. I knelt and dug at it with my hands.

"What is it?"

I felt something metal against my fingertips and wrapped my hand around it. I pulled and pulled until out popped another golf club.

"Who would bury a club in the sand?" Justin asked, brow furrowing.

I shrugged. "Angry golfer?"

We both laughed.

Eric called over to us. "What are you two doing? We should have finished this hole already. We're holding everybody up."

My cell phone rang from the little pocket in my golf skirt. I took it out and saw it was the sheriff calling. I handed the errant club over to Justin as I answered it.

"Hey," the sheriff said.

"Hi, can I call you back? I'm just in the middle of something." I frowned as something about the club Justin held bothered me. There were bits of something dried on the blade that for some reason made me queasy.

He said, "Sure. I'm calling to let you know about the autopsy report. Jeremy died from blunt force trauma to the head."

"Really?" My stomach started to clench.

"Yup, looks like something metal with a thin edge was smashed into the side of his head. It left quite an indentation."

Bile slowly rose into my throat as Justin swung the club around and said, "It's a six iron." He gestured to me. "Hey, it has the same color grip as your clubs, Andi."

I swallowed. "Um, Sheriff, I think I may have found the murder weapon."

CHAPTER FIFTEEN

AFTER I CALLED LOIS to tell her the situation, she jumped into action and had everyone in the clubhouse organized to put her plan into place. She had the groups after us diverted to the fifth hole, claiming there was some kind of pipe burst on the fourth hole, and credited all the golfers with a one-under for the fourth hole to keep the play even. Which meant the tournament ended up with seventeen holes instead of eighteen. But since we were all playing for charity and for fun, no one seemed to mind.

As that was happening, the sheriff arrived with Deputy Marshall. He had the deputy stringing police tape around the sand trap and taking pictures, while he got busy grilling me.

"Please don't look at me like I put the club there," I said.

"I'm not." The sheriff shook his head and ran both hands through his hair. He must've left his office in a hurry without his hat. "This is just getting worse instead of better, Andi. Tell me how your six iron ended up here with what looks like traces of hair and blood on the blade."

I said, "Technically, it's not my club. The clubs belong to the hotel. We loan them out. Lots of guests and staff members have used these clubs."

"At this point, I don't think that matters. It's a hell of a coincidence, don't you think?" The sheriff's eyebrows were arched all the way to his hairline, his expression incredulous. "Your ex-boss. He ruined your life. He ends up dead on an island all the way across the country where you're now living. The murder weapon is a golf club that you've used on more than one occasion. And to top it all off, the murder weapon is found buried in a sand trap on the golf course on the same day you just happen to be golfing in a tournament."

"When you put it like that, it sounds really bad," I said.

His voice rose up an octave. "It *is* really bad, Andi. Haven't you figured that out yet?"

"Of course I've figured it out, or I wouldn't be having nightmares about Jeremy's smashed-in face!" I matched his pitch and raised him a few arm-flails.

Eric, Lane, and Justin, who had been talking to Deputy Marshall, all turned to look at me.

The sheriff took my arm and moved me away from the sand trap and prying eyes and ears.

"Okay, I'm sorry." He dropped his hand and blew out a frustrated breath. He lowered his voice. "I got a call from the feds. They're on the way."

My breath quickened. "The FBI is coming here?"

He nodded.

"Why?"

He shrugged. "They wouldn't say, but obviously there is more to Jeremy's murder than we know or can guess. I matched the cigarette you gave me to the butt I found by your patio.

Definitely the same Russian cigarettes. So, whoever broke into your place was probably the smoker. You were definitely targeted."

"How would they have known what suite I was in? No one would've given that information out to some random stranger."

He shook his head. "He may have followed you around. Got to know you. And the fact that you leave your blinds open..."

I glared at him. "Don't you dare bring that up again."

He put his hand up. "I'm sorry."

"A while ago, I did feel like I was being watched. I brushed it off as paranoia."

"Well, I'm thinking you weren't paranoid," he replied.

I shivered and rubbed my hands over my arms. "I just don't see the connection between some Russian man breaking into my place and Jeremy Rucker."

"Did Rucker ever do any business with Russians?"

I shook my head. "No. The majority of our clients were local. There was a couple who had ties to Japan and the UK, but no one in Russia." I thought about the SIM card and wondered what kind of information I was going to find on it. Maybe Jeremy had been involved in something bigger than the embezzlement we knew about. If the FBI was involved, that made sense.

Sheriff Jackson put a hand on my shoulder and squeezed softly. I had a strong urge to sink into his arms. If we'd been alone, I might've caved. As it was, with everyone looking, I kept my distance. So did he.

He waved to Justin. "You and Andi found the club. I'm going to need both of you to come down to the station to make a formal statement. Justin, I'll need to take your fingerprints for exclusion purposes. Andi's are already on file."

"Sure, Sheriff," Justin said.

We rode to the station with the sheriff. He sent Justin with Deputy Shawn to be fingerprinted, and I followed the sheriff to the witness room.

He set up his camera, and I repeated my story of the night Jeremy came to the hotel. How much I'd drunk, who I was with, when we left the clubhouse, Jeremy grabbing me and threatening me, Daniel's subsequent arrival, their altercation, the sheriff's arrival and departure. Then I covered how Daniel and I went to my suite and passed out on the bed together. I still didn't mention about waking up at around three and Daniel not being in bed with me. It wasn't relevant. I didn't believe for one minute that Daniel had murdered my ex-boss.

This time, the sheriff also asked about the break-in of my suite. It was good that he was recording the connection before the FBI arrived. Better to be proactive instead of reactive in a situation like this. It was too easy to assume I had a motive to kill Jeremy, and someone was conveniently connecting it all together. In fact, I was really the one and only suspect. Jeremy didn't know anyone else here. I was his sole link to Frontenac Island.

If I had been investigating, I would think I was the one who'd killed Jeremy Rucker, with the help of my big, strong boyfriend, Daniel Evans, whom I'd coerced into helping me. It made sense.

When we were finished and had left the witness room, the sheriff said, "I hate this."

I gave him a small smile. "I know." I lifted my hand, intending to touch him with it, but I remembered myself, remembered where I was, and let it drop.

But he grabbed my hand and held it tight.

We stood like that in silence, holding hands, for what seemed like forever. As if we'd had a flash of realization hit us at the same time, we dropped hands and moved apart. I turned and walked out of the station, heart racing and head swimming.

Realizing I was a logical prime suspect for murder and holding hands with the hunky sheriff, all in one short visit to the station, was too much for my overwrought imagination.

I didn't have a ride back to the Park, but I didn't want to go back in and ask for one. I set out in the direction of the hotel. The walk would do me good. I crossed Market Street and then decided a little detour past Chocolat wouldn't hurt. A box of salted caramels would do my soul some good. Maybe not so great for my hips, but definitely would make me feel better.

I popped a creamy, salty caramel into my mouth as I walked up Main Street. It was a beautiful day, but the briskness of an early fall was in the air. Too soon the leaves would begin to turn vibrant colors. Desserts, coffee, and other things would be pumpkin-spice flavor, and I would be turning a year older. Fall was always bittersweet for me.

As I approached Frontenac Island Bubbles Soap Co., I noticed Ben and Corey sitting outside the shop selling their soap from a table. They both smiled when they saw me.

"Gorgeous Andi. We haven't seen you in forever," Corey said as he flipped the bedazzled scarf he was wearing over his shoulder. "I love your skirt."

I looked down, realizing I was still in my golf attire. "Yeah, I've been busy."

"Golfing, apparently," Corey said with an amused lift to his handlebar mustache.

Ben grabbed a paper bag from the table, dropped in a dark-colored bar of soap, and handed it to me. "On the house. You need to take some time for yourself."

"Thank you." I was touched by their generosity.

As I put the paper bag into the same hand I used to carry the one from Chocolat, something across the street caught my eye. Actually, it wasn't *something*—it was *someone*. A man leaned against the side of the building near Victoria's Pub, smoking a cigarette. He lifted his hand to take a drag of it, and his head turned toward me.

I'd seen him before.

His gaze caught mine, and he immediately dropped his cigarette and turned to walk the other way. I dashed across the street, nearly getting hit by an old man on a tricycle. He tooted his horn at me, flipped me a rude gesture, and then continued on his way.

I reached the spot where the smoker had been standing and searched the ground for his cigarette. It was still smoldering. I picked it up. It had a gray filter and smelled exactly like the other Russian cigarette I'd smelled before. I dropped the butt and rushed after him.

As I ran, images of people zipped by in my mind, as if I was flipping through a photo album or going through slides. The slide show stopped on a beautiful sunny day at the Flower Festival. The day I'd won my giant unicorn. Or more accurately, a man named Ivan won the giant unicorn for me at the ball-toss game. During the same time, my suite had been broken into.

The Russian cigarette-smoking man was Ivan.

Ivan ran across the street, maneuvering around a few bikes, a couple of runners, two skateboarders, and one horse-drawn carriage. I followed Ivan, careful not to step into the large dung piles left by the horses. After a quick glance over his shoulder to look back at me, he ducked into the fish-and-chips shop on the corner near the docks.

After a few seconds, I dashed into the shop. I quickly searched the small, cramped space and didn't find him. Then I noticed there were stairs leading up to the rooftop patio. I ran the steps two at a time, nearly knocking over a poor young server, and burst out onto the open deck.

Ivan was nowhere to be found. How could he have simply disappeared? What did he do, jump in the water? That would have been crazy.

I walked to the edge of the patio and noticed there was a shed one floor below. Ivan could easily have jumped onto the shed's roof from where I stood. Next to the shed was the marina. One of the dock platforms bobbed up and down as if someone big had just run across it.

I went back down the stairs, out of the fish-and-chips shop, and around to the marina. There were four separate piers that housed six boats on each side, for a total of forty-eight boats. Some of the boats weren't docked. I couldn't go looking into every boat, but I could walk down each pier. If he was hiding somewhere, I might find him.

This was one of those times where I was chasing after dangerous evidence and I should call the sheriff. I pulled out my phone, my finger on the button, when I saw something move near one of the big yachts docked down the last pier. I ran toward it to find a bunch of gulls feasting on some fish guts someone had left on the dock.

"Damn it."

Intending to call the sheriff immediately, knowing full well I was being a fool running around down here on my own, I turned with my phone to my ear. Just as the sheriff answered, I ran into a solid object. I stumbled backward, my purse and bags flying out of my hands to land on the dock. And right before I tumbled ass over tea kettle into the water, I saw Casey Cushing's smiling face.

"Oops. I hope you can swim."

Chapter Sixteen

THE WATER WAS AN icy punch to my whole body all at once. The cold stole my breath as I floundered to the surface. It was hard to swim upward, kicking my feet, with only one hand to help propel me. My other hand clutched my phone, which I would not let go of for anything. My phone was my lifeline. Thankfully, I was a decent swimmer. I was on the swim team in high school, but that was long ago. It was also swimming in a pool. Where I knew others were around to save me from drowning.

Breaking the surface, I inhaled a deep breath and got a mouthful of oily water with it. I sputtered, cursing up a storm. Even I was shocked at what came out of my mouth. I dog-paddled to the dock where Casey was crouched, holding out a hand.

"Let me help you," he said.

I handed him my phone first, and he set it down next to my purse, and then reached down to grab me. He wasn't very strong, so basically it was just me kicking and hefting myself out by sheer anger alone.

Once I was on the dock, I flopped onto my back and took in a whole bunch of much-needed air. Casey loomed over me.

"I'm so sorry. I didn't mean to scare you."

"You pushed me," I said between chattering teeth.

He had the nerve to look appalled at the suggestion. "I would never. You ran into me and tripped backward. I tried to grab you, but it was too late."

I sat up, swiping the heavy wet globs of my hair from my face with a shaking hand. My whole body quivered from the cold water followed by the brisk breeze that blew over me. Casey offered his hand to get me to my feet, but I refused. I pushed up to my knees then to my feet. My clothes were stuck to me like cold, wet glue and probably left nothing to the imagination. At least Casey was decent enough to grab my purse, bag, and phone and hand them to me.

As he looked me over, I could see he was fighting a smile. I must've looked like a drowned raccoon in a super short skirt. My makeup was running down my face, and my hair was plastered to my head. I glared at him.

"What are you doing down here, anyway?" I asked, trying to sound demanding, but some of the oomph was lost by the chattering of my teeth.

"I often come here on my dinner break and look at the boats. I'd love to buy one, one day," Casey said, as if we were friends and he was sharing his deepest secrets.

I didn't believe him. He was here, exactly at the same time as Ivan. That was no coincidence.

Ivan probably broke into my suite. To do that, he'd have had to acquire information about me first. Who better than Casey

Cushing to supply my living arrangements? Casey was a petty man who disliked me and had unfettered access to the hotel.

But why? Was he paid to supply the information?

"A little out of your price range, don't you think? What with all the bills you have from taking care of your mom."

He didn't respond to that, but I saw him flinch. He dodged my question and asked, "What are you doing here? It looked like you were searching for something."

"I was. A man. A big guy with short dark hair, mustache, wearing a gray suit jacket and jeans." I eyed him sharply. "Maybe you saw him."

"Nope, I didn't see anyone until you came barreling out of nowhere." He pursed his lips. "We should really get you a towel or something. You're shaking like a leaf."

We walked down the dock together—well, Casey walked in front, and I shivered with every step behind him—until we reached Main Street. Before we took another step, the sheriff's SUV came to a squealing stop right in front of us.

Sheriff Jackson jumped out and ran over. "What the hell happened?" He took me in, his gaze going everywhere, and I realized he was looking for injuries.

"She fell off the dock," Casey said, as innocent and wholesome as apple pie.

"You pushed me," I corrected.

The sheriff's gaze zeroed in on Casey, who actually took a step back. "I did not push you." He pleaded with the sheriff, "I didn't push her, I swear."

Sheriff Jackson put an arm around me and directed me to his SUV. Once there, he opened up the back of the jeep and pulled out a big blanket. He draped it around my shoulders and then wrapped me in it, rubbing my arms as he did so.

"How did you know where I was?" I asked.

"Lucky guess. You called, and when I answered, I heard the word 'swim,' then a huge splash, then nothing."

He helped me into the front seat and then shut the door. I could hear him talking to Casey.

"Do we need to have a little chat?" he asked.

I saw Casey shaking his head vehemently. "It was an accident. I swear to you."

I wanted to cry out, "Liar!" but I honestly didn't know for sure, and I'd keep my mouth shut until I knew differently.

The sheriff jumped into the jeep. He turned the heat on as we drove away from the marina.

"Didn't Casey want a ride?" I asked.

The sheriff shook his head. "He said he'd walk."

I had my doubts, considering the look on Casey's face as we drove away. My heart skipped a little as I glanced across the console toward the sheriff. His face was a mask of concern and determination. I liked that he protected me, even in small ways, like not giving a ride to a man who may or may not have pushed me into the freezing water unprovoked. The gesture warmed me inside. And right now, I needed all the warmth I could get.

When we arrived at the hotel, I asked him if we could go in through the side door instead of the main entrance, so I could avoid the lobby. I didn't want anyone to make a big fuss over me or ask a bunch of questions. I just wanted to get out of these wet clothes and get warm.

Once inside my suite, I handed the blanket back to the sheriff. "I'm going to have a hot shower."

I didn't wait for his response, assuming that he would wait for me. He probably had a ton of questions about what happened on the docks.

I peeled off my clothes in the bathroom, turned on the water, and stepped in under the hot pulsing spray. Relief was instant, and I groaned loudly, not caring if the sheriff heard me or not. I stayed under the cleansing spray a long time until the stink of algae and fish and the sticky feel of oil left my skin. I probably looked like a pink lobster now.

I got out, dried, wrapped myself in my fluffy white robe, and returned to the living room. As I'd guessed, the sheriff had waited. He'd been inspecting my collection of books and pictures on the shelves, his hands folded behind his back. He turned when I came into the room. He gestured to the table.

"I made you some tea. I could only find something peach flavored, so I hope that's okay."

I sat on the sofa and picked up the cup, enjoying the warmth of it in my hands. I took a sip and sighed. "It's wonderful, thank you."

He paced a little. "You have some decent books."

I almost laughed because it didn't quite sound like a compliment. "Thanks. I like crime novels."

"Yeah, that doesn't surprise me." He pointed to the picture of Miss Charlotte. "Who's that?"

"Miss Charlotte. She was my nanny growing up. She was my best friend."

He looked surprised at that. "You didn't have a lot of friends?"

I shook my head, sipping my tea. "Not really. My parents isolated me a bit, I think. I went to a private school and was enrolled in dance classes, and sports, and piano lessons. But nothing really stuck. No one really stuck. Not until college when I met Ginny."

He sat down next to me on the sofa. "You grew up rich?"

"My parents were pretty well off. I know that now. At the time, I wasn't aware of it. We never discussed money in our house," I said.

"Were? They're not—"

I shook my head. "No, nothing like that. They're still alive, but I don't see them often. They live in Hong Kong."

"Oh." He rubbed his hands together. He looked really nervous for some reason. "So, why were you at the marina?"

I set my teacup down. "Don't get angry, but I'm pretty sure I found the man who broke into my suite."

He shook his head. "And you followed him."

"Yeah, kind of chased him, really. I was walking back to the hotel, and I spotted him near the Victoria smoking, and I recognized him from the Flower Festival. He was actually the guy who won that," I pointed to the giant unicorn in the corner, "for me at the ball toss. He'd said his name was Ivan. Anyway, he saw that I'd noticed him, and he ran, so I ran after him. He lost me near the marina, so I went looking."

He shook his head again.

"I didn't have the chance to call when I was chasing him, but I called you when I was at the marina…"

"What if it had been this guy you ran into and not Casey? Do you think he would've just pushed you into the water?"

"No."

He frowned. "I can't keep you safe when you actively chase danger."

"I didn't realize you were trying to keep me safe," I replied.

"Of course I am. It's my job. Not only to keep *you* safe, but everyone on this island." He got to his feet. "You're the key to this case, though. I think whoever killed Jeremy is keeping tabs on you. And I can't follow you around 24/7."

I glanced at the blanket that was now folded on the sofa. "Have you been sleeping in your jeep to watch my suite at night?"

He stared at me without answering.

"Why don't you just get a room here? You would be so much more comfortable." I was teasing him a little, and he knew it.

"It's too expensive. I can't afford to stay here. Not on my salary."

I smiled. "Okay, I won't go running toward danger, if that helps."

His eyes narrowed.

"I promise this time." I held up three fingers together. "Scout's honor."

"Like you were ever a Girl Scout." He shook his head, but there was a ghost of a smile on his lips. "Okay, that's a good start. And you've told me everything of importance, right? You aren't hiding anything helpful to this investigation?"

I shrugged. "Nope. You know everything I know."

He eyed me for a long moment, and I thought for sure he would call my bluff. But he didn't. He picked up the blanket and headed to the door. "How about you stay put for now and get some rest?"

"Yeah, that's probably a good idea, but unfortunately I can't. We have the big banquet at the hotel tonight, out in the gardens. Lots to do." I walked him to the door. "When I get back, I'll make sure everything is locked up, and I'll even keep my lights on, so you can get a good night's sleep."

"I'll get a good night's sleep when this is all over. Until then…" He tipped his head and left my room. I shut the door and locked it behind him, knowing he would wait until he heard the lock engage.

I went back to the sofa, got comfy, and then reached for my laptop that wasn't there. I needed a replacement. I couldn't do any of my sleuthing without a computer. I called Ginny and asked where I could get a cheap laptop and phone. For the time being, I gave her the short version of how my phone had ended up in the water at the marina. I refused to give up on my old phone. Maybe I could find someone who could fix it. In the meantime, I took out the phone's SIM card and tried to dry it out as best I could.

I hadn't told her about my dinner conversation with Clive Barrington yet. Mostly because I was still working on the problem in my own head. If I wanted to stay here, it wouldn't help to have Casey or Lane or Samuel find out that I had somewhere else to go. For various reasons, I was pretty sure all four of them would put me on a plane to Hong Kong and throw me a party to send me on my way. I loved Ginny, but she was the world's worst secret keeper.

Ginny hooked me up with her phone guy who turned out to be a twentysomething woman with pink dreadlocks. Rowan worked out of the basement of her parents' house. She assured me she could fix my phone and then gave me a replacement that I could pop my old SIM card into, and it would have all my contacts and phone numbers on it. Which was good, because I honestly couldn't remember anyone's phone number. I don't know how anyone had memorized phone numbers before cell phones. I'd probably done it when I was young, but I didn't get my first phone until I was thirteen. Now, kids as young as eight carried cell phones.

Rowan also hooked me up with a refurbished laptop for only $150. I took my new purchases, returned to my suite, and ordered room service. I sat out on my patio with the laptop to dig up some dirt on Casey Cushing, because I knew he was hiding something.

CHAPTER SEVENTEEN

I STARTED WITH A simple search for *Casey Cushing*. Eleven profiles popped up on six social media accounts. I found one profile on a business site and scrolled through it first. The contents were the usual sales tools of working professionals, listing current and past employers and education. Nothing in there was surprising or unusual, except he listed an interest in collecting.

I clicked on a couple of the social media accounts. He'd posted nothing but inspirational quotes and photos from the hotel. I went through his friends list, which consisted mainly of profiles for people who worked at the Park Hotel, some old school friends, and his mother, Penny. I clicked on her account, which was much more revealing.

There were a lot of pictures of her with Casey. Many were photos of her hospital stay and then her recovery from the surgery at home. Pictures of Penny using a walker, then a cane, and pictures of Casey doing chores around the house. Despite my feelings about him, these photos really did look like he loved and cherished his mom. A couple of months back, she had posted a picture of one of her medical bills with a big frowny face drawn on it. The bill was $62,876.57. It looked like she'd had one or two complications during her surgery.

Shortly afterward, there was a photo of Penny with a PAID IN FULL stamp on the bill and a huge grin. That was a lot of money to acquire in such a short time. The paid bill was posted around the same time that my suite had been broken into. Casey hadn't even returned to work yet. Where did she get the money?

My cell phone rang, startling me. The ring tone was loud— church bells. It was Ginny calling.

"Are you on your way?" she asked the second I answered.

"On my way where?"

"To the banquet hall. It's already six o'clock, Andi."

I looked at the clock on the computer: 5:05 pm. I guess I'd forgotten to set the clock to the right time zone.

"Oh, yes, I'm on my way."

"You forgot, didn't you?"

"No."

After I hung up with her, I rushed into the bathroom to do something with my hair and slather on some makeup. I put on a clean-cut, black pantsuit with an emerald-green blouse. I slipped on comfortable heels since I was going to be on my feet the entire time, grabbed my purse, and rushed out the door. I made it to the hall in record time. It had only taken thirty minutes to get presentable.

I met up with Ginny and Lois, who both gave me a look, then we proceeded to make sure everything was in place and running smoothly for the banquet. There was another day of golf tomorrow, then a gala in the evening. The event usually raised tens of thousands of dollars for various charities, but it was a ton of work to make everything run smoothly.

It was basically all hands on deck, so there were about ten of us on staff making sure everything happened without a hitch. Casey and I were in charge of getting everyone seated. Lois did the introductions of the various speakers, and Ginny orchestrated it all behind the scenes. I loved seeing her with her little headset and clipboard, calmly and efficiently handling everything. People thought she was flighty and disorganized, but they were wrong. Ginny was a powerhouse. Exactly like her mother in that way.

Casey and I worked opposite sides of the room, making sure people were seated at their assigned tables before the speeches began. Once we were done, we stepped out of the room into the main corridor. I was all set to march over to him and ask him point blank if he'd ransacked my suite and sold information about me to pay his mother's hospital bill, but his cell phone rang, and he answered it. He stepped around the corner to talk, and I slid up along the wall to eavesdrop.

"I've been waiting for your call." He paused to listen. "Of course I can get it for you...I won't take any less than ten thousand this time...I think she suspects, but she doesn't know for sure...I'm not worried about her. I can deal with her if I need to."

There was a longer pause while he listened for a while. Then, before he disconnected, he said, "I'll call you when I get there."

I heard some rustling and a long silence, so I risked a peek around the corner. Casey was walking down the corridor to one of the exits. I followed him without a second thought.

Once outside, he jumped into one of the hotel golf carts and took off down the hill to the village. I couldn't follow him in another cart. He'd see me plain as day. I needed something that would be less obvious. I spotted one of the bicycles that the hotel loaned out to guests and grabbed it.

I pushed off, wobbling for a second before I found my balance. Actual bike-riding was nothing like spin class. I rode the brakes all the way down the hill, keeping to the darkened pathway. At first, I thought he was going to the marina. But when he got to Rose Lane, he turned left. I followed him, nearly wiping out in front of Daisy's Pet Hotel when I took the corner too fast.

Casey drove to Market Street and then took a left. I had no clue where he was headed. He turned right onto Clover Avenue, which led to a residential area. Then he took another right, then another, and parked near a big industrial-looking building.

I waited in the shadows. He got out of the golf cart, walked to the gate, and punched a number into the keypad. The gate buzzed, and he opened it and went through.

I ran to the gate to sneak inside before it could close, but I was too late. The gate shut and locked with an audible click. I looked through the metal bars to the sign over the door. The building was a storage facility that rented out individual storage units. I rattled the gate and then looked down the way to see if there was another entrance. There wasn't. I had to go over the gate if I wanted to get in.

Grabbing the metal bars at the top, I stretched my leg up, hooked my foot into the crossbar, and pulled myself up. Then I reached over the bars and swung my leg over until I was straddling the top bar. This was not easy to do in a pair of dressy trousers. They were made for strutting through an office with style, not climbing over a metal fence and skulking around.

I made it. Once over the gate, I ran down the rows, hoping to find Casey before he disappeared inside one of the units. I walked down the first row. No sign of him. I turned the corner and went down the second. I paused when I heard some movement four units down on the right.

As I stood there pressed against one of the metal doors, I thought about what to do. What if Casey was meeting with the Russian? What if the Russian had a gun? I reached into my purse and pulled out the pepper spray. I put my finger on the trigger and crept along the cement lane until I reached a unit marked with the number 18.

Light flooded from under the roll-up metal door. Someone was definitely inside. I could hear him moving around.

I pressed my ear to the door, hoping to hear voices. If I could stay outside and record the conversation, it would be much safer. But I didn't hear anything. Either they weren't talking, or I couldn't hear the voices past the metal. I couldn't just stand out here. It was time to do something bold.

Crouching, I put my fingers under the edge of the door. Then, counting under my breath to three, I pushed the door up on its rollers as hard as I could. I rushed into the unit with my pepper spray aimed and ready to use.

I didn't know who was more startled, Casey or me. He actually made a low squeaking sound and tossed the thing he'd been holding in his hand onto the ground. I bent to pick it up and stared at it, not completely sure how to associate what I was looking at with any kind of nefarious activity. It was a stuffed toy, shaped like a crab, with green, blue, and brown fur.

I looked up, and my eyes nearly bugged out of my head. Casey was surrounded by plush toys. Bears, horses, dogs, cats, and more. I spotted a unicorn and an octopus. Hundreds of them piled on shelves all around the storage unit.

"What are you doing here?" Casey demanded.

"Ah…" was all I could get out.

He came over and snatched the stuffed crab from my hand. "You have to be careful with him. He's worth a lot of money."

"I'm not sure what to say," I replied.

"Did you follow me?"

"Yes."

"Why?"

"Because I thought…because I'm not sure what I thought, to be honest." I looked around some more and splayed my hands. "What is all this?"

"My Beanie Baby collection."

"I heard you on the phone at the hotel talking about money." I took a step toward one of the shelves, trying to take in the massive number of plush animals on the shelves.

"I was talking to a buyer." He held up the crab. "For this guy. The buyer will pay ten grand for him."

I turned and gaped at him. "You're kidding."

"I am not." He glared at me. "I sold Peace Bear for seven thousand, Millennium Mint Bear for five thousand, and two rabbits—Hippity and Hoppity—for six thousand each."

"Wow. I had no idea." I reached for a cute dog, but Casey slapped my hand.

"Don't touch them."

It was then I noticed he was wearing gloves.

I looked up and spotted a blue bear in a glass case. I pointed to it. "How much is that one worth?"

"Right now, she's worth about seventy-five thousand. But I'm holding her until the market reaches about a hundred thousand."

I shook my head, but now the quick payoff of his mother's medical expenses made sense. "You've been selling these to pay your mom's bills."

He nodded, and his eyes narrowed. "But how did you know about mom's bills?"

"Social media. You'd be surprised what you can find out about a person."

He sighed. "I hate parting with them, to be honest. Mom bought them all for me when I was a kid."

"That's a lot of stuffed animals."

"I was a sickly kid. I didn't get outside much. My mom bought them to be my friends." He picked up one of the cats, brought it up to his face, and smelled it.

"I'm sorry," I said, shaking my head. "Wow, I couldn't have been more wrong about you."

"What did you think I was doing? Selling drugs or something?" He put both hands on his hips and glared. "And why were you following me, anyway?"

"I thought you'd sold information about me to the man who broke into my suite recently." I turned and looked at him. Might as well face the truth.

He scowled as if I had honestly offended him. The expression was totally different from the faux offense he displayed when he knew he was being a jerk. "I can't believe you'd think I would do that. We don't particularly like each other, but you're calling me a thief and a criminal."

"Yeah, I'm sorry." I sighed. "It's been a rough few days."

He came over and handed me the little gray striped cat he'd been holding. "Here."

"Ah, I thought I shouldn't touch any."

"Oh, this one isn't worth anything. I heard you've been missing your cats. You can have her."

I took the toy and smiled, feeling touched by the odd offering. "Thanks, Casey."

"Just don't tell anyone about this." He gestured to the hundreds of Beanie Babies. "I've heard of people getting robbed and murdered for them."

"I won't." I put the little cat into my purse, along with the pepper spray I still held. My cell phone buzzed, and I looked at it. It was a text from Ginny.

Where the hell are you?

"It's Ginny, wondering where we are," I said. "Can I catch a ride with you back to the hotel? I rode one of the bikes here, and I'm not sure I can ride it back up the hill. It was enough trouble to ride down."

CHAPTER EIGHTEEN

THE NEXT MORNING, I woke up to the chiming bells of my phone's ring tone. Groggy, I flopped an arm toward my bedside table and fumbled for the phone. I dropped it onto the floor and then had to lean over the bed to grab it. I managed to answer before the call went to voice mail.

"Hello?" I said without opening my eyes.

"Why am I looking at security footage of you breaking into All Goods Storage last night?" *Sheriff Jackson. Man, that guy gets around.*

I rolled onto my back. "Well, I really wasn't breaking in. I was sort of with someone."

"Andi," he replied in that tone he often used that was half-warning and half-exasperation. I imagined he was either rubbing a hand over his chin or running it through his hair. "What the hell?"

"Are you going to charge me with breaking and entering or something?"

He sighed. "No, but stop pressing your luck."

"I was following a lead, but it didn't pan out."

"You are a civilian. You shouldn't be following leads of any kind."

"Don't you ever get tired of telling me that?" I smiled to myself, hoping he heard it in my voice.

He chuckled, and it made my belly tighten. "Yes, I do get tired of it."

As a private citizen, I could investigate anything I wanted. We both knew that. Of course, breaking and entering was a crime. So there was that. "Did you check out the registrations at the marina? Anybody named Ivan?"

"No Ivan listed anywhere."

I sighed. It had been a reach anyway. It wasn't like he'd register under his own name.

Sheriff Jackson said, "I checked the other hotels, inns, and even the bed-and-breakfast places. None of them have anybody named Ivan registered now, and none had anybody named Ivan registered any time this year. It's not a common name, apparently."

"He's not a figment of my imagination."

Sheriff Jackson inhaled and exhaled for a long time before he said, "I know."

I checked the time. It was early, but if I didn't get my butt in gear, I would miss my tee time. "I've got to go."

"All right. Have a good day," he replied. "No shenanigans."

"Did you really say 'shenanigans'?" I laughed.

He disconnected.

I made it to the course on time, and we all teed off. I crossed my fingers and made a quick wish for the game to finish up uneventfully. The last thing I needed was to be digging more evidence out of sand traps.

When Lane and I were out of earshot of Eric and Justin, I leaned over to him. "Are you going to be home this evening?"

His eyebrows went up, probably thinking I was hitting on him until he remembered our previous conversation. "Yeah. Should be."

"I'll bring pizza and beer."

"Sounds good to me."

The rest of the game, I thought about Jeremy, wondering what he'd gotten himself involved in. More than embezzlement, for sure. None of our clients would murder him for stealing their money. The firm's insurance would pay the money back. He supposedly had big gambling debts. Maybe he owed some bad people a lot of money. The insurance wasn't likely to repay that kind of debt. I was hoping whatever was on his SIM card would reveal all.

After the golfing was over and my other duties were complete, I commandeered a golf cart and headed down to the village. I picked up a large pepperoni pizza and a six-pack of beer on the way and knocked on Lane's door. He lived in a townhouse in one of the newer neighborhoods that I'd never been to before. Despite the island's relatively small size, there were quite a few places I hadn't seen.

The door was opened by a handsome elderly man with a gorgeous head of white hair. He smiled. "Hello, dear."

"Hi. I'm Andi. Is Lane here?"

He turned his head and shouted, "Lane! Your girlfriend is here!"

"Oh, I'm not his—"

Lane came running. "Thanks, Pops."

He grabbed my arm and pulled me into the house and through the living room to the stairs leading down to the basement.

Once we were in his apartment, for lack of a better word, I set the pizza and beer down onto a table. "Is that your grandpa?"

"No," he said as he flipped open the cardboard box and grabbed a slice of pizza. "That's Ed. He's my roommate."

"But you called him Pops." I looked around for a place to sit. Every spot seemed to be covered with clothes, books, or video-game cases and controllers.

"It's just what I call him. He likes it." He shoved some clothes off a chair and gestured for me to sit. "When I first got the job at the Park, I didn't have a place to stay, and rent was way too high for me on my own. I think it was Nancy who told me Ed needed someone to live with him, pay some rent, and look after the place."

I grabbed a slice of pizza and sat. "That's pretty cool. Smart, too. You're probably saving a lot of money."

He nodded. "I do all right." He folded the slice in half and shoved it into his mouth. While chewing, he went over to the desk set against one wall. There were two monitors on it, a keyboard, a mouse, and an assortment of other electronics I couldn't name. "Let's see your SIM card."

I grabbed my purse, took out my wallet, and handed Lane the tiny plastic card in the baggie. He took a smartphone from his desk, popped open the card tray, and slid the card into.

"It's password protected," I said.

He powered up the phone, and the password screen flashed on. He plucked a cord from a desk drawer, connected it to the phone, and then plugged it into the side of one of his computers.

An icon with the words "New Device" popped up on his screen. He right-clicked on it, and a list of options was offered to open the information on the device. Lane clicked on something labeled "trikart." The second that happened it seemed like a million pop-up windows started to explode on the screen. His hands were like lightning on the keyboard and mouse, clicking buttons and typing words. I didn't know what was going on.

"The software is reading the encryption and trying to find a way in," he said by way of explanation. "It might take a bit."

"How long's a bit?"

"Twenty minutes to four hours. It's hard to say. Depends on how serious the encryption is."

"I can't hang out here for four hours. I have to attend the big gala tonight at the hotel." I checked the time. The gala started at eight, so I had maybe two hours to play with before I had to get back, get dressed, and look presentable. The last thing I wanted to do was worry Ginny and Lois about whether I would arrive at all.

Lane gestured to the TV. "We could play some video games."

I looked at him, realizing just how young he was. I glanced at his other computer monitor. "Can I use that, while this is going on?"

"Oh yeah, for sure."

I pulled up a chair to the other computer and typed in the remote web address for the hotel. I had access to the system, and I had used the remote access to the hotel computer before from my suite. It felt a little weird logging on from Lane's computer, but I wasn't doing anything illegal.

The login screen popped up, and I typed in my user ID and password. After a few more clicks, I had access to all the registrations and check-ins and check-outs at the hotel for the past few years. I wasn't sure if the man who'd introduced himself to me as Ivan had stayed at the Park, but I could definitely check to see if he had and whether we had a last name for him.

I typed in the dates for the Flower Festival and typed in the name Ivan. There couldn't possibly be a whole bunch of Ivans who had stayed at the hotel. During the relevant dates, no one using Ivan as a first name showed up in the system. I shouldn't have been surprised. He likely had stayed at another hotel on the island or even one of the B&Bs.

He might have stayed on a boat. Maybe that was why he had run toward the marina. He could have had a boat docked there. Boats docked there were required to register, similar to staying in a hotel. Registrants had to provide a full name, legal address, and form of photo ID.

Just as I was pulling out my cell phone to call the sheriff, Lane clapped his hands together in excitement.

"We're in."

"Now what?" I asked as I rolled my chair closer to his.

His fingers flew across the keyboard, and then he was dragging files across the screen with the mouse. "Looks like some accounting spreadsheets." He clicked on the first file.

A spreadsheet opened. It looked like a simple cash account ledger. Name, the amount of money coming in, and the money being paid out. These were individuals—Jones, Singer, Cassell, Hassad, Matsu. I recognized some of the names as clients of my old law firm, Alcott, Chambers & Rucker.

Then the amounts: $10,000 in, $70,000 out, $50,000 in, $80,000 out. Where the money was going, I couldn't tell. Jeremy might have had an offshore account in Switzerland or the Caymans. The types of accounts we'd often suggest to our clients to secure their wealth. There were other numbers in the ledger, and they could've been account numbers, but I couldn't know for sure.

There were a lot of other files, random entries over the past five years. I asked Lane to click on the next file. There were different names listed and fewer of them. A third file had only two names, Jones and Sorrentino.

It was a nightmare simply looking at all of it. My stomach churned from seeing the actual evidence of Jeremy's crimes in front of me. After I'd heard that Jeremy had been arrested, I'd often hoped the charges were false, that he was innocent. But deep down, I'd known all the things they'd told me were true. The firm's partners would never have reacted the way they had if there had been even a shred of falsity to the claims.

Seeing everything laid out, names and numbers, made my head spin. I pushed my chair away and stood up to pace the room. It felt like I might be sick. Lane must've seen my distress, because he pushed a bottle of water into my hands.

"I take it this is not information you wanted to see."

I shook my head. "You can't tell anyone you saw this. And I mean no one, Lane."

He nodded. "I won't."

"Can you print this all off for me? Then wipe it from your computer?"

"Yeah, I can do that."

I sat on the sofa, on top of the clothes stacked there. "I'm just going to sit for a minute while you do that."

Thirty minutes later, I had a stack of fifty pages in a manila envelope. I headed back to the golf cart I'd borrowed from the hotel. I had watched Lane as he wiped the information from his computer and gave me back the SIM card. I made him promise for the millionth time to not talk to anyone about this. After seeing what was on the card, I felt nervous about getting Lane involved, too. The information was dangerous. Jeremy had been killed over it.

After I went through everything, I planned to hand it all over to the sheriff. He could forward it to the FBI. I just hoped it was enough to take me off the suspect list.

I slid into the cart, started it, and pulled away from Lane's house. After a block, I noticed another cart behind mine. I wasn't sure where it had come from. I hadn't noticed any carts turning onto the road behind me. I turned left, and the second cart followed. Then I turned right, and it followed.

On the next turn, I sped up. I expected the cart to speed up behind me, but it didn't. I made another left turn, pulled over, and saw the second cart drive by at the regular speed limit. I didn't recognize the cart or the driver.

My heart pounded in my chest. Closing my eyes, I leaned against the steering wheel. After taking in a few deep breaths and letting them out to calm myself, I put the cart in gear and drove onto the road.

My hands were shaking by the time I pulled into the hotel's lot. I parked and got out of the cart. As I was crossing the lot, I noticed another cart parked nearby. It looked very similar to the one that I'd seen following me. I walked over and checked it out. I didn't know what I was expecting to find. A sign that read "I'm following Andi Steele because I killed Jeremy Rucker" would've been helpful.

"What are you doing?"

The voice startled me, and I propelled forward and hit my forehead against the roof of the cart. Turning, I rubbed at my forehead to see Daniel half-smiling/half-frowning at me.

"Nothing."

"Why were you looking into that cart?"

I shrugged. "I've been thinking about buying a cart. I was just checking out how roomy it was up front."

"Why do I get the feeling you're feeding me a line of crap?" Daniel asked, cocking his head.

"I don't know." But I laughed. "Are you here for the gala?"

He nodded. "I'm early, but I'm meeting with Lindsey beforehand."

He meant Mayor Lindsey Hamilton. "Cool."

We walked into the hotel together, and he gave me a side-eye. "Why do I get the feeling you're avoiding my texts? I've sent several since that night."

"I'm not avoiding you. I actually drowned my phone." I showed him my replacement.

"How did you do that?"

"Don't ask. It's a long, wet story."

He chuckled. "Okay, I won't pry." He grabbed my hand. "I'll see you later? There's supposed to be music at this thing, so I hope you'll save me a dance or two."

"Of course."

He leaned down to press a kiss to my lips. It was quick, and I didn't respond. When he pulled back, I could see the hurt on his face.

I was in some kind of deep trouble. I couldn't let him be pushed into danger he hadn't signed up for. I was protecting him by pushing him away. But it was more than that. Kissing Daniel would've sent the wrong message. I'd tried to avoid my feelings for Luke Jackson, but they kept creeping up. When this was all over, I would tell Luke how I felt about him, even if I ended up moving to Hong Kong. I wasn't sure what was going to happen. It would probably end up a disaster. But I was quickly becoming accustomed to disasters.

CHAPTER NINETEEN

BACK IN MY SUITE, I set the envelope on the table. I wanted desperately to go through the pages, but I wouldn't make it in time to the gala, and that would definitely be pressing my luck with Lois and Samuel. I'd get ready first. Then, if I had some extra time, I would take a look at these pages. If not, then after the gala.

I took out the blue, off-the-shoulder, tea-length dress that I hadn't gotten much use out of at the Flower Ball. I swept my hair back into a low bun, backcombing a bit on top to give it some height. I'd been neglecting my hair since I relocated to Frontenac Island. That was another thing I'd have to fix.

After I put on some light makeup, plum lipstick, and shellacked my hair with hairspray, I checked the time. I had about thirty minutes before time to go. I slid my shoes on and laid my clutch on the table by the door so I could just snatch it on the way out.

I sat on the sofa and slid the papers from the envelope. As I went through them, I wrote down the names, amounts, dates, and account numbers in my notebook, to try to make sense of it all. Halfway through the fifty pages, it started to look more like money laundering than embezzlement. Or possibly a combination of the two. Jeremy was definitely using clients' money to filter through some other accounts. But also listed was money from people who weren't clients. And there was a lot more money going out than coming in. Just from the first twenty-five pages, I was looking at over two million added up in my notebook.

"Jesus, Jeremy, what were you thinking?" I said aloud as if he could hear me.

I leaned back on the sofa just as my phone buzzed with a text from Ginny.

YOU'RE AN HOUR LATE!!

I set the pages aside on the table and jumped to my feet. I grabbed my purse from the foyer table and went out the door. Thankfully, the ballroom was only a five-minute walk from my suite. When I arrived, music cascaded out from the doors, while posh tuxedoed men and gorgeously gowned ladies wandered in and out, holding flutes of champagne.

Ginny pounced on me. "Why are you so late?"

"I'm sorry." I took her in. She looked stunning in an ankle-length, pink lacy dress with spaghetti straps. Her hair fell in romantic ringlets down her back. "I lost track of time."

"Doing what?"

I shrugged. "Just stuff."

"I would've forgiven you until I saw Daniel here. So I know that wasn't it."

Ignoring her innuendo, I took in the gala. It was packed with smiling people, and the ambiance and decorations were spectacular. I'd been to many fund-raisers when I was with the firm, but none of them had this much appeal.

She gripped my hand. "This is the biggest event I've planned solo. Lois has always been involved. I need it to run smoothly."

"Ginny, it'll be fine. You did an amazing job. I'm sure Lois is very proud of you."

"I hope so."

I almost told her about the situation with my parents and Club Paradise and Clive Barrington, when over her shoulder, I spotted a handsome man in a black tuxedo, brown hair slicked back, carrying two flutes of champagne. He was walking our way. Took me another moment to realize it was Mr. Minsky from the boat ride the morning we'd found Jeremy on the beach. He looked different all dressed up.

"You disappeared on me."

Ginny turned, and her smile was instant. She took the offered glass from him. "Thank you, Victor." She glanced at me. "Do you know Andi Steele, our concierge?"

Victor tipped his head. "Yes, we've been talking. Ms. Steele has put together what will surely be an amazing fishing expedition tomorrow for a few of my colleagues and me."

"I hope the weather holds," I said. "I'm hearing rumors of a big storm rolling in."

"I'm not scared of a little wind and rain. I'm Russian."

Ginny laughed.

I didn't. There was something in the way he'd said that...it sent a shiver down my back.

"May I tempt you with a dance, Ms. Steele?" He held out his hand to me.

I hesitated, and I thought Ginny was going to elbow me in the ribs along with the stink eye she was already giving me.

"Of course." I took his hand, and he placed it in the crook of his elbow as he led me onto the dance floor.

The band was playing an instrumental version of some old pop song that couples were waltzing to. Victor put his hand on my waist, took up my other hand, and whisked me onto the floor. He was very good. I wasn't the greatest dancer, but he made it seem easy for me, which I appreciated.

"Do you like working for the Park Hotel?" he asked while he spun us around the floor.

"Yes. Very much."

"Ever thought of working for someone else?"

My eyes narrowed. "Are you offering me a job, Mr. Minsky?"

"Please call me Victor."

"All right, Victor."

"I've heard you are very resourceful and tenacious. I could use a person like that."

"Doing what exactly?" There was something about this conversation that settled wrong in my belly.

"I could add a good lawyer to my team."

"I'm not a practicing lawyer anymore."

"But I could help make you one again. I know the right people to make that happen." He smiled.

I frowned. "You seem to know a lot about me."

"When I see something I want, I tend to do a lot of research on it. Make sure I know every angle, every vulnerability."

My hand flinched in his, and he gripped it a little tighter. Not hard enough to hurt, but enough that he got my attention.

"Well then, you'd know that I'm happy where I'm working now."

He nodded. "Yes, I imagine working here is fun. Such great people. Nice, friendly people."

The music ended, and we came to a stop at the edge of the dance floor. He let my arm drop and then gave me a little nod. "Enjoy the rest of your evening," he said, then walked away.

I watched him leave and felt unsure and uneasy. We'd had nothing more than a conversation, but somehow it felt like it'd been a bit of a threat.

Before I could react, Daniel found me. "Want to dance?"

I nodded. "Sure."

The band played a ballad, and Daniel held me close as we swayed to the music.

"Do you know Victor Minsky?" I asked him.

"Not really. We've met only once before, years ago, when I was still in the construction business with my father."

"What do you think of him?"

"He's a decent businessman. His company is profitable."

"Yeah, but what do you think of *him*?"

"He's arrogant. I've heard he can be ruthless in his dealings."

Over his shoulder, I spied Ginny laughing with Victor. She touched him on the arm and beamed up at him. He leaned into her ear and said something, and then they were leaving together, his hand resting lightly against her lower back.

I didn't like it. Something was wrong with him. I didn't trust him.

"I've got to go. I'm sorry," I said as I pushed out of Daniel's arms.

He grabbed my hand to stop me. "You're always running away from me. Why is that?"

"It's not really about you," I said honestly.

"Is it about the sheriff?"

I just looked at him. From day one, Daniel had been concerned about Sheriff Jackson. Jealous even. I guess I hadn't seen what he'd seen until recently. "Yes."

He dropped my hand. "I can't say I'm not upset about it."

"I'm sorry, Daniel. I really am. You're a wonderful man."

"Except Luke is the better man." He leaned down and kissed my cheek. "I've enjoyed getting to know you, Andi. Keep out of trouble."

I gave him a small smile. "I'll try."

He turned and walked away from me, heading for the exit. I watched him go, feeling sad about the situation. I definitely didn't want to hurt him, but the relationship wasn't going anywhere. Pretending otherwise would've hurt him more in the end. Better to end things before hearts were truly broken. Probably mine.

Speaking of hearts, I had to find Ginny. When she liked a guy—and she had certainly shown all the signs when talking with Victor—she tended to throw all caution out the window. There was definitely something wrong with him. I didn't know exactly what, but my instincts were usually right.

I left the ballroom, searching for them. I spotted Casey talking with someone at the food table and approached him. Since last night, we were sort of in a better place with each other.

"Casey."

He turned to me, eyebrow raised.

"Have you seen Ginny?"

"Yeah, she left with Mr. Minsky, I believe." He gestured toward the main lobby of the hotel.

"Thanks." I quickly made my way to the lobby. Through the big windows, I spotted Ginny with Victor heading toward the parking lot.

I rushed across the lobby and out the doors. Just as I came around the sidewalk, I saw a golf cart pull away with Ginny in the passenger seat. I swore it was the same cart that had been following me before.

"Damn it." I took out my phone and called her. The call went immediately to voice mail, which meant she had her phone off.

I didn't know what to do. I couldn't prove that Ginny was in any kind of trouble or that Victor was a dangerous man. But I felt it when I danced with him. Looking into his eyes was like looking at a shark. He'd done research on me, and I wanted to know why. Not because he wanted to offer me a job. Every instinct I possessed told me he was up to something else entirely.

A gust of cold wind blew up, flipping the hem of my dress and yanking at my hair. I looked up and over the bluff and saw dark clouds rolling in from the lake. Flashes of light charged from within the clouds. There was definitely a storm coming.

I returned to the hotel, the wind at my back, pushing me forward. Everything suddenly felt overwhelming. I was way over my head here. I needed to gather all the evidence I had and go to the sheriff. Whatever this was, I couldn't do things on my own any longer.

Instead of returning to the gala, I took the corridor to my suite. When I reached the door, a crack of thunder rumbled from outside and made me jump. I didn't like storms very much. When I was little, I used to hide under my bed until the thunderstorms passed.

I opened my door and went inside. I walked toward the living room, then froze. It was dark inside my suite, and I knew I had left the lamp on in the living room. I had been in such a hurry to get to the gala that I hadn't turned it off. I knew this for sure.

A flash of lightning from outside my patio doors illuminated the room briefly. A mighty rumble of thunder came within seconds. During that flash, I had seen the coffee table was bare. I'd left the envelope and papers on it. They were gone.

As I looked slowly around the room, my heart thundered in my chest. I took in a deep breath, trying to control my heart rate. The sweet smell of Russian cigarette smoke filled my nostrils. It came from inside the room. I swallowed and weighed my options.

I could turn and make a run for the door. I might be able to get out and call for help. Or I could dash forward and get out the patio door. It was closer, but the table was in the way, and I'd be running out into the stormy darkness. In this weather, no one else would be outside.

Another flash of lightning bathed the room in bright white light. Movement caught my eye from my right. The crack of thunder exploded around me just as he pushed me. He yanked my purse from my hand. My knees hit the table with a thud, and I landed on the floor as the patio door flew open. A large black form dashed out and vaulted over the cement berm surrounding the patio, disappearing into the storm.

I got to my feet. The heel on my left shoe was broken, so I kicked both shoes off. I went over to the patio and looked out, but he was long gone. I closed and locked the door, and then I turned the lamp by the sofa on and looked around. The envelope and the printouts were indeed gone. He got what he'd come for.

I inspected the rest of my suite and noticed a few things moved and out of place. I had a feeling he'd been looking for the SIM card, and I had interrupted his search. I sighed and sunk down into the sofa, lamenting the loss of my purse. That was the second phone I'd lost in a couple of days, and all my ID.

I rested my head on the back of the sofa, still trying to regulate my heart rate, then reached into the bodice of my dress, under my bra and pulled out the SIM card. Thank God I'd had the presence of mind to remove it from my wallet and stash it somewhere no one would search. I needed to get it to the sheriff right away.

When I got to my feet, my heel slipped on something. I reached down under the sofa and grabbed whatever it was. It was a piece of paper. It was one of the printouts, page fifty. I set it on the table and looked at it, going over the names and numbers. I was hoping it would be enough for the sheriff to see how valuable the data on the card was.

Then my gaze landed on one very familiar name. Minsky. And a payout of $500,000. That was a whole lot of motive for murder. And Ginny, my best friend in the world and dearer to me than any sister I could ever have, was his captive.

CHAPTER TWENTY

I RUSHED INTO MY bedroom, unzipped my dress, and squirmed out of it. I couldn't be running around outside in the wind and rain in a ball gown. I pulled on a sweatshirt and a pair of leggings. I slipped my feet into a pair of running shoes, grabbed my jacket from the closet, and headed to the door. I had to find the sheriff and tell him about Minsky.

There was another long string of lightning flashes, then the instant crash of thunder that rattled the paintings on the walls. The storm was getting closer. I reached for the doorknob just as it shook from someone knocking hard on the door.

I let out a little yelp.

More knocking. "Andi!"

Relief surged through me. I threw the door open to see Sheriff Jackson. He walked into my suite, already talking, "I've been looking for you. Casey said you went running off."

"I went to find Ginny."

"I got a hit on Ivan."

"You did?"

"He left his prints on the golf club that killed Jeremy. Ivan Sorokin, no fixed address. He's got a rap sheet for assault and a few other violent crimes, mostly in the Detroit area."

"He was here again."

His brow furrowed. "What?"

"I came into my suite. It was dark in here when I got back. I know I'd left the lamp on. I'm sure he was looking for the flash drive Jeremy had mentioned. I interrupted him."

His eyes widened, and he gripped the back of the sofa. "He was in here with you?"

I nodded.

"Did he hurt you?"

"He just pushed me to the ground so he could run."

His gaze did a frantic sweep of my body.

"I'm okay, just banged up my knees."

He released the breath he was holding. "Did he find anything?"

I made a face. "Yes and no."

He shook his head wearily. "You've been keeping evidence from me again."

I showed him the SIM card. "I found it in my framed picture of Ginny and her family."

He took it from me. "Do you know what's on it?"

I nodded. "Yeah, it was encrypted, but I had someone break the encryption and print off what was on it. I had the printed papers on the table. He took those."

Sheriff Jackson pulled a plastic bag from his jacket pocket and slipped the SIM card into it. He sealed it then folded it and put it into his front jeans pocket for safe keeping. He then scrubbed his face with both hands. He was beyond frustrated, and this time, I didn't blame him.

"What was on it?"

"Names and numbers. I recognized some of them as clients of our law firm. It looked like Jeremy was laundering money and using client funds to do it," I said. "Which probably explains why the FBI is interested, too."

He blew out a breath. "Enough money worth killing for?"

I nodded. "Oh yeah."

"Did you recognize all the names?"

"A few were definitely clients. The others, I didn't know." I unfolded the piece of paper I'd stuffed into my jacket pocket. "Here. Look at the last name."

He read it. "Minsky?"

"Victor Minsky. He's the CEO of Minsky Manufacturing out of Detroit. He's here on the island. I thought he was attending the fund-raiser weekend, but it seems he had ulterior motives."

"What?" He gaped at me, his head jerking. "Is he here in the hotel?"

"He was." I shook my head. "He left. With Ginny."

I could feel the tears brimming in my eyes. I'd put the most important person in my life in danger. Unknowingly. But still. Victor Minsky had come here for me, because of something I didn't know I had.

The sheriff reached for me, grasping me by the upper arms. "This isn't your fault, Andi. You did not do this. Jeremy did this. He hid that card in your picture frame. This is his fault. Understand?"

I gave him a quick nod, but the tears still threatened to fall.

He lifted his hands and cradled my face. "It will be okay. We will find Ginny."

He grabbed his radio. "Marshall, you there?"

There was static, then the deputy answered. "Go ahead."

"What's your 10-20?"

"Ferry dock. Getting sandbags in place. The waves are huge, Sheriff. I've never seen anything like it."

"We have a possible kidnap in progress. All deputies on lookout for Ginny Park. Thirty-two-year-old female, long brown hair, green eyes."

He looked at me. "What was she wearing?"

"Long pink dress," I said.

He asked, "What about Minsky? What does he look like?"

"I'd say in his forties. Your height and build, brown hair, blue eyes, wearing a black tuxedo."

Sheriff Jackson got back on the radio and relayed the pertinent information to Deputy Marshall.

"Do you want me to pursue?" the deputy asked.

The sheriff wiped his mouth. "No. Continue with emergency procedures."

"Copy that."

He clipped his radio back onto his belt. "Looks like it's just you and me. I can't ask anybody to come over from the mainland in this weather."

I gave him a small smile and grabbed his hand. We left my suite together.

As we walked toward the lobby, there was another series of lightning flashes and a deafening crack of thunder that shook the glass on the windows. I jumped. Several people in the lobby yelped. Then we were plunged into darkness as all the lights went out. That caused a few more yelps, and I heard some screams coming from the ballroom.

The sheriff took out his flashlight and turned it on. "Do you know where your emergency kits are?"

I nodded and pointed toward the corridor to the back offices. I ran up to the front desk. Lane was working it, using the light on his cell phone to find his way.

"I need the key to the maintenance office," I said.

Lane handed me a ring of keys from the desk. "What should we do?"

"Make sure we get people out of their rooms and in one central location. Bring everyone down to the ballroom. Almost everyone is down there anyway, and there's food and drink. Lois and Eric will be there."

While we rushed forward, the front-desk staff jumped into action as scared, bewildered guests started wandering into the lobby. The spa and other stores were already closed up for the night.

I directed the sheriff to the maintenance office. I opened the door, and we gathered all the lamps and flashlights we could find. We headed toward the ballroom. As we passed the front desk again, I left a lamp with them.

When we arrived at the ballroom, I was surprised to find it less chaotic than I'd assumed it would be. It looked like Lois and Eric and other staff had taken control of the situation. I found Lois and handed her a lamp.

"Thank you." She lit it up, and then looked around, past me. "Where's Ginny? Isn't she with you?"

I glanced at the sheriff. I wasn't sure what to tell her.

"We're looking for her," he said.

She frowned at me. "Andi. What's wrong? What's going on?"

I told her everything...from Jeremy's money laundering, the SIM card he hid in my picture frame, the related break-in, Victor Minsky's involvement, and finished up with the fact that Ginny went willing with him somewhere.

She grabbed my hand. "Do you think he'll hurt her?"

I wanted to say no, but, honestly, I didn't know. Ivan had killed Jeremy, but Jeremy had been a direct threat to Minsky and probably had stolen Minsky's money.

"I don't know," I said, on the verge of tears again.

"We won't let that happen," the sheriff promised. "We'll find her. It's a small island. There are only so many places they could be."

I was about to say something else to soothe her fears when a huge crash came from the lobby. It sounded like glass breaking. The sheriff, Lois, and I went running toward the sound. Two big trees had fallen through the windows on one side of the lobby. Glass littered the floor, fallen leaves blew around the room, and one of the sofas that had been near the window lay on its side, cushions wet and spotted with debris.

Everyone in the lobby jumped into action. Gloves and brooms and large trash bins were passed around. I started to sweep some of the smaller glass fragments from the lobby floor when Lois joined me, taking the broom from me.

"I've got this. Go find Ginny. Find my girl."

I hugged her and then looked for the sheriff. I found him helping to move the other sofas away from the windows, his boots crunching on shards of glass. Once he was finished, he rushed over to me and took my hand without a word, and we left the hotel and went out into the storm.

The wind and rain whipped my body as we ran to the sheriff's jeep. I was drenched instantaneously. He started the vehicle and turned the heater on full blast.

"We'll stop at the station. We need better gear for this weather."

He drove out of the parking lot and onto the main road that led down the hill to the village. He drove slowly while the wind pummeled the side of the jeep, rocking us back and forth. Trees lining the road bent against the gale, and I clenched the dashboard, anticipating that one of those trees might be ripped out of the ground and smash into us.

As we drove down Main Street, I could see the damage the storm inflicted on the village. Bicycles lay on their sides on the sidewalk. Garbage from the trash bins blew around the street, making tiny tornadoes with leaves and other debris. When we passed slowly by the wharf, I saw waves lashing at the wooden pier, engulfing the boards with every surge. Water ran along the streets. If the waves got any higher, Main Street and surrounding businesses would certainly flood.

Before we turned toward the station, Sheriff Jackson stopped in front of the Swan Song bar. He slid the jeep's transmission into park. "Stay here. I'm going to check on Marshall and the others."

He opened the door, and the wind whipped it out of his hand. He jumped out and then pushed the door closed. As he went toward the ferry dock, the wind nearly knocked him on his butt. Bracing against it, he marched on.

The jeep rocked back and forth as I waited, reminding me a bit of a boat on waves. I put my hands in front of the heater vents. I'd yet to get warm. I'd never seen a storm like this before. Not firsthand, anyway. Only in videos of hurricanes that had battered the east and south coasts.

Another bright flash of lightning filled the sky, exploding over the water. The show would have been pretty if it wasn't so frightening. More rumbles of thunder followed, making me jump again. Yet another lightning flash illuminated the street, and that was when I spotted a man trying to board up the windows of his shop. He was having trouble. He couldn't hold up the wood and pound nails at the same time.

I jumped out of the jeep and ran across the street to help. I grabbed one of the boards and held it up across the window. The proprietor, an older man, thanked me as he pounded nails into the wood. The roar of the water pulverizing the shore drowned out all of his pounding. I grabbed another board and put it up. It slipped a little on my left, but another man came to help.

As the board was secured, I glanced briefly at the man in the rain jacket who had rushed to help. When he turned to look at me, I recognized his face under the dark hood.

"Don't say anything," Ivan warned.

"Where's Ginny?"

"She's safe. For now."

"If you hurt her, I swear to God, I will kill you."

He chuckled. "I don't doubt it."

I glanced over my shoulder and spotted the sheriff working with Marshall and the others to sandbag the shore.

Ivan saw me looking. "Don't bother calling out to him. He wouldn't be able to hear you, anyway."

"What do you want?"

He slipped something into my jacket pocket. "We'll call you with a time and place."

"For what?"

"A trade. The card for Ginny."

"How do I know she's not already dead?"

"She'll be the one calling you."

I wanted to reach over and strangle him or punch him or anything to make him hurt, make him bleed. I gritted my teeth. "You are going to regret this. I promise."

He smiled again. "You are everything she said you'd be."

I frowned, wondering who he meant. Ginny? Had Ginny told them I'd fight tooth and nail for her?

"Wait for the call. And when it's time, you come alone. If we even get a whiff of sheriff lover boy around, Ginny will be the next one tossed over the bluff." Then he turned and disappeared down the road into the wind and rain and darkness.

CHAPTER TWENTY-ONE

THE SHERIFF RUSHED UP to my side as I helped put up the last board over the shop window.

"What are you doing out here?" he shouted over the gale-force wind.

"I had to help."

He looked at the shop owner. "You okay, Nick?"

Nick nodded and then hustled off to get into his own vehicle parked in front.

"You're soaked through." He put his arm around me, and we ran back to the jeep. Once inside, he pulled away from the curb, and we turned toward the station. He parked in front of the red-brick building, and together we ran inside. Thankfully, the lights were still on.

Deputy Shawn was manning the station. He whistled when we came in, sopping wet, making puddles on the tiled floor as we both removed our jackets. I was careful to keep the burner phone Ivan had given me hidden in the pocket. The last thing I needed was for it to fall out onto the floor in front of the sheriff.

"You two look like drowned rats. Especially you, Andi."

I really didn't have the patience to put up with this crap. "Hey, Shawn?" I flipped him a rude gesture.

He laughed. "Wow, kitty has claws."

The sheriff glared at him. "Get on some gear and go out and help Marshall at the docks. There are still lots of sandbags to be filled and stacked up. Then make the rounds in the village. Be sure everyone is securely hunkered down for the night."

Shawn was smart to shut his mouth and not make any more comments. Sheriff Jackson's body language told me he'd probably knock him down if he even made a peep. I figured Shawn could sense that, too, because he went in the back and came out with rain gear and rubber boots.

Once he was dressed and out the door, the sheriff gestured to me. "C'mon around back. You can get out of those wet clothes and into something warm and dry."

I followed him to one of the back rooms, which looked like a storage area. This was where the station kept all the extra uniforms, heavy snow jackets, and other equipment like generators, backpacks, and what appeared to be riot gear with shields and battering rams. I even spotted a couple of tasers. I wanted to ask if he'd ever had to use that stuff but decided it probably wasn't the best time.

The sheriff grabbed a gray sweatshirt and pants from one of the shelves and set them on a bench. "They might be a little big, but they'll do the trick."

He grabbed some for himself, and without further conversation, he started to unbutton his shirt.

I turned around and tried to pull off my sweatshirt, but it got stuck halfway up my arms. I struggled a bit, realizing I probably looked like a fool fighting with my clothes.

I heard the sheriff chuckle softly. "Do you need some help?"

I sighed. "Yes, please."

I could feel him move in behind me. I was extremely aware of the heat of his body near the cold skin of my back.

"Lift your arms straight up," he said.

I did as he instructed, and he pulled on the sopping fabric of my sweatshirt until he was able to peel it over the tips of my fingers. He laid it down on the bench and handed me the dry gray sweatshirt. I pulled it over my head, feeling instant warmth on my skin from the soft fuzzy inside of the shirt.

I looked down at my drenched leggings and realized these wouldn't be easy to pull off, either. So, I moved over to the bench and started rolling the waistband down. The sheriff had quickly turned to face away from me. I continued to roll the fabric until it came over my hips and butt, and then I sat down and peeled the rest down my legs.

As I pulled the sweatpants on, I glanced over and got a quick peek of the sheriff in his boxers before he pulled his pair of sweatpants up. He glanced over his shoulder at me, and I quickly looked away, embarrassed I'd been caught checking him out. If his roguish grin was any indicator, he didn't mind one bit.

"Better?"

I nodded and ran my hands over my arms. "Much."

"Good. I'll make us some coffee. It ain't Starbucks quality, but it should do the trick."

I followed him into the kitchen. It was fully stocked and, by the looks of it, would probably last a week or more. While he got busy making the coffee, I lowered myself into one of the chairs at the table. What I really felt like doing was curling up into a ball on the floor. I was tired. My body still shook, not only from the cold but from the shock of what we'd just been through. And I was worried about Ginny.

I believed Ivan's promise about Ginny being unharmed. He didn't seem like a man who would hurt a woman unnecessarily. *Unnecessarily* being the key word. I believed he would hurt her if he felt he needed to. That I didn't doubt. Victor Minsky, on the other hand, I didn't know anything about. He was definitely a cold fish, a predator. Would he hurt Ginny? Probably. Given the chance.

The sheriff returned to the table with two steaming cups of coffee, sugar, and fake creamer.

"If you want something fancy, I think there's some toasted-marshmallow mocha creamer in the fridge."

I eyed him with a little smile. "Who drinks that? You?"

He sipped the coffee. "Maybe. I'll never tell."

I took a drink. It burned my tongue a little, but the warmth soon spread down my throat and warmed my belly. I wrapped my hands around the cup and relished the heat.

"Once the storm dies down a bit, we'll go out and look for Ginny."

I nodded, trying not to give anything away. Ivan had said no sheriff, or Ginny would get hurt. I believed him. I didn't want to put her life in even more danger than it already was. I just had to get the SIM card back before the sheriff locked it up as evidence.

"Any ideas about this Victor Minsky? Did he fly in? Or come in on the ferry?" he asked.

"I'm pretty sure he flew in."

"Didn't you say you saw Ginny in a golf cart?"

"Yeah."

"Did you get any plate number?"

I shook my head. "No, I'm sorry."

"That's okay. It's probably registered under a different name, anyway."

"Do you have a computer?" I asked. "We could do some snooping on Victor. Maybe we can figure out where he would go on the island."

He nodded and then stood. "I'll go get my laptop. I'll be right back."

The second he left the room, I was up and out the door and back into the storage room. The sheriff's jeans were draped over the bench. I grabbed them and rammed my hand into each pocket to find the evidence bag. I got it and shoved it into my bra just as the sheriff called my name.

"Andi?" He came into the room carrying his laptop. "What are you doing?"

"I was looking for aspirin. I have a headache. I thought I had some in my jacket."

"Your jacket is out front." He studied me.

"Right." I nodded.

"I'll get you something for your headache."

"Thank you."

He waited at the door for me to exit the room, then followed me back into the kitchen. He set the laptop onto the table, then went to the cupboard to get me some pain medicine.

While he did that, I opened the laptop, went into a browser, and searched for *Victor Minsky Michigan*. His company page and profile came up, as well as several newspaper articles about his humanitarian and charity work. I kept scrolling, but nothing jumped out.

The sheriff handed me a couple of pills and some water.

"Thank you."

"Anything?" he asked as he slid a chair over next to me.

"Nothing important. The usual business stuff."

I typed in *Ivan Sorokin*, just for interest's sake. I wasn't expecting anything because I didn't imagine this guy had a social media footprint. I couldn't imagine him updating his daily status with skullduggery or sharing photos of his crew. As I suspected, all that came up was a page about some famous Cassock in the 1800s and a Russian figure skater.

The sheriff pulled the laptop toward him and clicked on the portal for a law enforcement network. He logged in. I tried hard not to memorize the keys he typed before he plugged in *Victor Minsky*. Nothing popped up. No warrants, no rap sheet, no outstanding parking tickets. On the surface, he appeared to be an upstanding, law-abiding citizen.

There was another loud crack of thunder from outside that made me jump again. The sheriff put his hand on my arm. "Don't like thunderstorms?"

"No. Hate them. I used to hide under my bed when I was a kid. I used to fear the sound would cut me in half."

"You're safe in here."

As if to contradict that statement, another crack of thunder sliced through the air. We could hear the front doors of the station rattling like chains.

I jumped again, turned, and grabbed onto the sheriff, hiding my face in the crook of his neck. He put his arm around me and rubbed his hand up and down my back. Like soothing a wild thing.

It felt good in his arms. Safe. Secure. Comfortable.

I lifted my head slowly, my cheek rubbing against his chin. I heard his breath catch as I turned my face to his. I stared into his eyes, seeing his pupils dilate, the blue of his irises darkening. Our lips were mere inches apart. I could smell the coffee on his breath, and I wondered what he would taste like.

He swallowed and licked his lips. I watched the tip of his tongue. Gnawing slightly on my bottom lip, I moved a little closer until we were a whisper apart. I parted my lips in anticipation of feeling his mouth on mine.

"This is so not the time," he breathed.

"I know. It's a bad idea."

"The worst."

I gasped as he pressed his lips to mine. The whole world started to spin, and I was spinning with it.

Then the sound of the front doors smashing open broke us apart.

We were both up and out of our chairs, running to the lobby to see Marshall come stumbling in. I didn't think it was possible to be as drenched as he was. He turned and struggled to pull the doors closed. The sheriff helped him. Once they were closed, the sheriff threw the bolt.

"It's bad out there, Sheriff. I've never seen it this bad," Marshall said as he peeled off his first layer of clothing and let it slap onto the floor.

"Are the sandbags going to hold?"

"I don't know."

"Okay, we'll have to hunker down here and ride it out." He looked at me. "I'm sorry, Andi."

I suspected he was apologizing for all kinds of things.

He said, "We can't go out and look for Ginny. It's too dangerous."

"It's okay. I understand."

"As soon as it dies down, we'll go. I promise."

I nodded.

"In the meantime, there's a cot in the back. You should try to get some sleep. I'll get you a blanket."

"Thank you," I said.

When he rushed into the back to get me a blanket, I grabbed my jacket from the chair I'd set it on to dry out. I had to take it with me to the back for when Ivan called. Once that happened, I didn't know how I was going to get away from the sheriff's prying eyes, but I had to find a way. Ginny was counting on me, and I would never let her down again.

CHAPTER TWENTY-TWO

I JERKED AWAKE, SITTING up, my heart in my throat, forgetting where I was and what I was doing here. When I remembered I was in the sheriff's station and why, I lay back down and took in a deep breath. I had been dreaming. Dreams of rough water and bleak darkness and death.

Ginny had been there. So had Ivan and Victor. And Luke.

I scrubbed at my face, not wanting to think about what had happened in my dream. I blinked up at the ceiling, listening for the sounds of the storm, but didn't hear any. It was still dark in the room. I reached over to the floor and found my jacket, pulling the disposable phone from the pocket.

It read 7:30 a.m. There were no missed calls or texts on it. Sighing, I slid it back into my jacket and then sat up. My bare feet pressed against the cold floor. I shivered, realizing my body still had the chills. I wondered if that cold would ever go away.

After putting on socks, I stood, then left the room and padded into the kitchen. The smell of toast and jam wafted to my nose, and my stomach grumbled in response, reminding me I hadn't eaten in quite a while. I saw that a fresh pot of coffee had been brewed, and I gratefully poured a cup and took a sip.

"Did you sleep?"

I turned to see Luke leaning against the door jam. He looked tired and worn, but still strong.

I smiled. "Yeah, a little."

"Good." He came into the room and put a hand on my shoulder and squeezed, then dropped it. "The worst of the storm has passed. It's still raining, but the winds have died down."

"I should get back to the hotel, help clean up. I imagine it's a madhouse there."

He nodded. "Eat something, and then I'll take you up."

"Thanks."

"We'll find Ginny," he said.

"I know. I have faith she's all right. I don't think Victor would hurt her. He's after his money, that's all."

He eyed me for a long moment, nodded again, and left. I was glad he didn't press me, although I sensed he knew I was keeping something from him. I trusted him implicitly. If I told him, I had no doubt he'd do his level best to save Ginny. The only thing that kept me from telling him was the fear that Ivan would do precisely what he'd promised if I told. I couldn't risk it. I needed to get back to my suite so I could figure out how to save Ginny without anyone getting hurt.

After I'd wolfed down the toast and snagged a banana, Luke drove me to the hotel. Main Street was a mess as we drove over fallen branches and garbage in the street. He dodged a couple of flags ripped from poles and strewn on the ground. At one point, we drove through a fairly deep puddle, and the water almost covered the wheels. But it was heartwarming to see people already out on the street, cleaning up, helping their neighbors keep their shops and livelihoods from being completely ruined.

As we came around the turn of Rose Lane, I spotted Daisy outside the kennels with a couple of other people cleaning up the street.

"Can you stop for a minute?" I asked Luke.

He pulled over so I could roll the window down. Daisy came over when she saw me.

"Quite the storm," she said.

"Are you good? How are Scout and Jem?"

She reached in through the window and patted my hand. "They're good. No problems. My place is a fortress. It was a lot of noise. I stayed with everyone the whole time."

I swallowed the panic that had been welling. "You are an angel, Daisy."

She shrugged and grinned. "It's possible."

"I have to go to the hotel to help clean up, but I'll be down soon to check on them."

"They're fine. I gave them some fresh tuna earlier and some catnip, so they are literally living the high life right now." She smiled and then turned to go back to the cleanup.

At the hotel, Luke parked in the lot, and we went inside together. He wanted to check out Victor's hotel suite. There was a lot of activity in the lobby. People sweeping floors and picking up debris. Mick from maintenance and a few others, including Nancy and Tina from the cleaning staff, had just finished erecting a plastic sheet over the broken windows. The electricity had been restored, so there was that buzz of activity with the front staff on computers, probably helping guests sort out their disrupted travel plans. There wouldn't be any planes or ferries leaving the island today.

Lois was in the middle of it all, directing and organizing cleanup efforts in addition to the hundreds of things she did every day. The moment she spotted us, she came over. She hugged me.

"Any news?"

I shook my head and grabbed her hand. "I promise she's okay, Lois, and we will get her back unharmed."

Luke glanced briefly at me and then looked back at Lois. "I want to check out Victor Minsky's suite."

She nodded. "It's suite 222." She handed me a master key, and off we went.

I unlocked the door to the suite, and we went inside. It was immaculate. Nothing had been touched or moved. It looked like no one had even been inside. I checked the bathroom. Everything was in place. No glasses had been used—they still had the wrapping on them. No soaps or shampoos opened. Towels were still folded neatly on the shelves, exactly as the housekeeping crew had placed them.

I came out of the bathroom to see Luke pulling open drawers—all empty. He went to the closet and opened the doors. It was empty save for the hangers and the ironing board nestled inside. The bed was untouched, unruffled, not a pillow or chocolate mint out of place.

"The staff wouldn't have cleaned the rooms yet, would they?"

I shook my head. "No, not with the storm damage last night. That would've taken priority."

Luke said, "It doesn't even look like he was ever here."

"That doesn't make sense. He checked in two days ago."

"He wasn't staying here, then. Must be holed up somewhere else. Probably the same place he's taken Ginny."

After we left the room and returned to the lobby, he said, "I need to take a drive to all the other hotels and B&Bs again. Maybe I'll get lucky, and someone will have seen him and Ginny."

"Okay. I'm going to stay here and help out as much as I can. If Ginny gets in touch, she'll call here."

He nodded and then went to touch my face, but as if remembering himself and where we were, in the middle of a crowded lobby, he quickly snatched his hand back. "We'll talk soon." He walked toward the exit.

"Oh, I don't have a phone, so if you want to reach me, you'll have to call the front desk."

"Will do."

The moment he was gone, I went back to my suite. I needed a shower and to change, and to think. There had to be a way to find Ginny. They would've ridden out the storm somewhere, like the rest of us had.

My suite hadn't sustained any real damage. Luckily, I'd closed my patio door before I left, so no rainwater had gotten in. The patio didn't get away unscathed, though. The table and chairs were strewn onto their sides. One of the chair legs was bent. One of the bushes next to the cement berm had been ripped from its roots and was now pressed up against the glass patio door as if it had tried to come in out of the storm.

I looked out at the grounds beyond my patio and saw sad destruction. Tree branches fallen, flowers and plants pulled from soil beds. There was even an umbrella from one of the outside tables at the restaurant rolling around the grounds from the wind. Beyond that, the water on the lake rolled, still looking a little wild, though thankfully, no twenty-foot waves like there had been last night. As I watched, I saw one of the ferries taking a test run out onto the water. I was surprised it hadn't been damaged in the docks.

I'd have to take care of the mess on my patio later. Right now, I needed to chase the cold from my body. I was still shivering. I wouldn't have been surprised if I ended up sick in the next few days. I jumped into the shower and turned the water as hot as I could stand it.

I lifted my face to the spray and tried to clear the cobwebs in my head.

I was missing something. I had to be. I felt like the answer was right in front of me, but I couldn't see it through the fogginess of my brain.

I got out, toweled off, and changed into chinos and a long-sleeved cotton shirt. I made some tea, carried it into the living room, and sat on the sofa. I opened up my laptop and typed *Victor Minsky Ivan Sorokin* into the browser. There was a connection between them, and Jeremy, and me. I knew there was. There had to be. It was pricking the edge of my memory. Poke. Poke. Poke. What was it?

I stood, frustrated, and paced the room, going through it all in my mind. The thread. It had started somewhere, but where? As I passed by my shelf, I noticed my framed pictures were knocked over, a couple of books on their sides. Maybe some wind had gotten through the crack in the balcony door.

I set them upright and then spotted a couple things on the floor. One was a crime novel, and the other was a postcard. I plopped the book onto the others and then picked up the postcard and leaned it against the framed picture of Ginny's family. My gaze had just brushed over the postcard as I was turning away, when I froze, then frowned and turned back to look at it again.

I picked it up, reading the words, reading the Russian scrawled at the top. It was from one of my clients at the firm. Beatrice Sorokin.

Sorokin.

Ivan Sorokin.

That couldn't be a coincidence.

I took the postcard back to the sofa. On my laptop, I typed in *Beatrice Sorokin Victor Minsky*. The first entry was a newspaper article that listed them both as contributors to a national children's charity, but their names were among thousands. The second was another article in *Business Weekly*. I clicked on it, and a photo of a group of people popped up. In it, Beatrice and Victor stood side by side. They had done business together.

I leaned back into the sofa and blew out a breath. I remembered my conversation with Beatrice when I'd first been suspended from the firm over Jeremy's embezzlement. She'd said, "He'd been stealing from me for years."

I'd thought at the time that she meant Jeremy was embezzling from her client accounts at the firm. But now I understood that Jeremy had also stolen even more of her money and Victor's money and deposited into some foreign bank account that they hadn't known existed. That account information was on the SIM card. Which was why they wanted it back. And really, they were entitled to it.

Leaning forward onto my elbows, I scrubbed my face. I couldn't believe it. I had a hard time reconciling the sweet elderly lady who had served me tea on several occasions after I walked her cute little dog with money laundering and Russian thugs.

I shook my head, trying to put all the pieces together. I looked at the computer screen again, making sure I hadn't misread, when my gaze landed on another link lower on the first page of entries. Two words popped out at me. *Sorokin* and *boat.*

I clicked on the link, and up popped a small story with a photo in a boating magazine. It was a short piece about a recent yacht purchase and the buyer. The photo was a smiling Beatrice Sorokin. Behind her was a large boat moored in a dock. The name of the boat was the *Magpie.*

I'd seen that name before. I'd seen that boat before.

I remembered it from when I went to talk to June at her shop a while ago. It had been docked in our marina.

Chapter Twenty-Three

THAT HAD TO BE where Ginny was. On the *Magpie*. Ivan had been hiding out there. Victor had stayed there instead of his suite at the Park. The boat must've been out on the water the day I followed Ivan to the marina. Hadn't there been a couple of empty slips when I was there?

I wondered if Beatrice was here on the island as well, watching me the whole time, waiting for Jeremy to show up to collect his little insurance policy. She must've known Jeremy hadn't given the information up to the authorities, or else they would've all been arrested.

I got to my feet. I had to get the jump on them. I knew where they were. They didn't know I'd figured it out. They thought I'd wait for their call, as Ivan had instructed.

I had to be prepared this time. I ran into the bathroom and grabbed the plastic bag with the SIM card inside. This was my trump card. Using pink duct tape—it was the only color I had—I strapped the baggie to my torso. I made sure it was secure and it wouldn't come off unless I wanted it to.

After slipping my jacket on, I put the pepper spray in one pocket and made sure the burner phone was in the other. I slid my arms into the dark-blue rain slicker Luke had given me last night. I patted the pocket where I had stuffed the taser gun I'd pilfered from the storage room when he wasn't looking. I knew how to use one. California could be a dangerous place, and I'd taken training classes.

I thought again briefly about telling Luke, but I'd be putting Ginny in more danger. No, I would go in and find Ginny on my own. They weren't expecting me. I could rescue her before they suspected anything.

I left the hotel through one of the side doors, feeling like I was sneaking out when Lois needed me, but it couldn't be helped. I commandeered one of the golf carts and took it down the hill to the village. It wasn't a smooth ride. The wind still whipped up every now and then, flapping at my jacket and making the cart rock, and I had to stop at one point to move a fallen tree branch to the side of the road.

I drove along Main Street, past the kennels and the stores and the people who were cleaning up, and parked near the fish-and-chips shop. I went around the building and peered at the marina. It was a shocking mess, to be sure. Some of the smaller boats had been washed up onto the docks, battered by the crashing waves and brutal winds. There were wooden boards floating in the water from broken hulls and busted rails. It was sad to see, knowing some people quite possibly had lost their livelihoods. But there was no sign of the yacht called the *Magpie*.

Where was the boat? There had to be other places around the island where boats could moor.

Instead of jumping back into the cart, I walked along Main Street to the ferry dock. I needed information and the two best sources, JC and Reggie, were helping in the efforts to repair the pier and the main building. It looked like some of the windows and doors had been blown in, and a few of the rigging poles on the pier had been bowed.

Reggie nodded in greeting when he spotted me. "Hello, Park Hotel lady. How are you this fine brisk morning?"

"Tired." I picked up the hammer he was reaching for and handed it to him. "How's the damage? Fixable?"

"Oh yeah. These docks are built to last. We've been here for forty years, and we'll be here another forty." He smiled. "How's the hotel?"

"Not bad. A few broken windows and downed trees, but nothing that can't be fixed."

"Exactly," he said with flourish.

"Hey, Reggie, I was wondering if there are other places to moor a big boat?"

"How big?"

I shrugged. "Luxury-yacht size."

His brow wrinkled. "Only a couple places for those. One on the north end of the island, and the other—"

"Below the bluffs at the hotel."

He nodded. "Yup, that's the one."

I remembered the ferry stopping in deep but calm water there after we'd spotted Jeremy's body on the rocky shore.

"How do I get there?"

"You'd have to take a boat out of the harbor and go around by water. Other than that, you could climb down the bluff from the hotel."

I frowned, not liking either of those options. Taking a step back, I let Reggie return to his work. I walked out toward the pier, wondering if there was a boat I could borrow. Not that I knew how to captain a boat. That's when I spotted someone familiar getting into one of the county patrol boats.

"Hey, Shawn."

He turned and frowned as I approached him. "The sheriff send you to bust my balls about something?"

"Nope. I was just wondering where you're going."

"Assessing the damage to the docks around the island. Why?"

"Because I need to get around to the mooring spots near the west bluff."

His eyes narrowed. "What's in it for me?"

I shook my head. "You can't just do a citizen a good turn?"

"Not when it's for you, Nancy Drew. You've screwed up my life enough already."

I couldn't really argue his point. So I shrugged. "What do you want?"

"I don't want to be transferred."

"That's not something I can change."

"Sure it is. You most definitely have the sheriff's ear, among other things."

"Fine. But you need to fix your attitude and how you behave. And you could do a better job, too. *That's* why you're being transferred, not because of anything I've said."

He held out his hand. "Deal."

I shook it, and he helped me into the boat. As he powered out of the harbor, the wind and rain picked up. I looked across the lake to see more black clouds blowing in our direction.

"Looks like we're in for it again," I said.

"Yeah, that's why I need to make this fast. Where am I taking you?"

"The mooring stations below the west bluff."

He gave me a funny look but didn't say anything. He steered the boat to the starboard and pushed the throttle so we were cutting across waves, pounding hard. I had to hang on or be catapulted out of the boat. I wondered if he was driving like this on purpose. He was kidding himself if he truly thought I was going to talk Luke out of transferring him off the island. Luke would do whatever suited him. Shawn should have known that.

As we came around the corner, I spotted the yacht immediately, backed up into the mooring station. It was too big not to miss. But I didn't want them to see me coming. How the hell was I going to get there undercover? Then I spied a little dock with a boathouse connected to it.

I pointed. "Can you drop me off there?"

His eyes narrowed again, but he didn't question me. I'd chosen the one person who really didn't care what I was up to. He steered the boat to the dock, and when the port side bumped against the pier, I stepped out.

"Thanks."

"Don't get yourself killed," he said as a way of a friendly parting, then reversed the boat and returned to deeper water.

I ran into the boathouse to take shelter as the wind lashed out, nearly knocking me off the dock and into the water. Through the broken window of the boathouse, I studied the *Magpie*. It was two-tiered, the cockpit being on top. I imagined the staterooms were below. Where would they keep Ginny? And how the hell was I going to get onto that boat without being seen?

Crouching inside the boathouse, I waited as more ominous clouds blew in, instantly plunging the world into darkness. I never thought I'd be thankful for another storm cell. With my dark slicker on, hood up, I didn't think I would be spotted crossing the stony beach by anyone having a quick glance out of the windows or off the deck. If someone was seriously looking, then I'd be spotted, but I had to take the chance.

As the first lightning bolt zipped across the sky, followed by the rumble of thunder, I left the boathouse and slowly picked my way across the stones. It was slow going, and I slipped twice as waves crashed up against the shore and sprayed water at me. When I reached the second dock, I crouched at the end and studied the yacht.

The lights inside the boat were on, so I could see any movement on board. I counted two people roaming about on the top deck. One of them was most likely the captain. I spotted another man on the lower deck. He came out from below, looked around, inspected the ropes tied to the dock, and then went back inside the cabin.

Now was my chance.

I jumped up onto the dock and ran down to the stern of the boat. I climbed over the railing then up the three steps to hide under the table bolted to the deck. Lightning flashed overhead, and when the thunder rumbled, I quickly stood up to take a peek into the main cabin.

I spotted Victor sitting on the curved sofa, drinking coffee and eating some kind of bread and preserves. There was a little bowl of fruit on the table in front of him. Movement caught my periphery on the right, and I saw Ivan walk into the cabin, also drinking coffee. They looked like two people having a casual breakfast on their yacht in the middle of a storm, and not ruthless mobsters.

I ducked down, realizing I would need to come along the port side to get to the stairs leading down to the staterooms.

Crouched with my back to the wall, I peered around the corner along the portside deck. It was empty. It was now or never.

Staying crouched under the windows, I crawled to the bow of the boat. I quickly looked inside the cabin again. No one was looking my way, and I snuck inside to the stairs leading down.

I walked down slowly, listening for noises, which proved more difficult than I'd hoped because of all the thundering that was happening overhead. There were four closed doors leading off the short corridor. I put my hand on one handle, turned it slowly, and opened the first door on my right. The room was unoccupied. I closed the door. I went to the next door. Taking in a deep breath, I opened it.

Ginny was sitting on the bed, and her eyes widened when she saw me. I put my finger to my lips, and she nodded.

I entered the room quickly and closed the door behind me. I rushed to the bed and hugged her.

"Are you okay?" I whispered. "Did they hurt you?"

She shook her head. "No. Everyone's been surprisingly pleasant. Considering."

"Considering they won't let you leave, you mean?"

"Yeah, that." She smiled. "What are you doing here?"

"Rescuing you."

Tears rolled down her cheeks. "I thought they were going to kill you."

"I'm resilient. You know that. I get knocked down, but I always get back up again."

Ginny smiled through the tears. "Sounds like that Chumbawamba song."

I screwed up my nose. "Oh, I hate that song."

"I know." She chuckled softly and wiped her nose with the back of her hand.

I gave her a little squeeze. "Okay, so the plan is to go up the stairs, then go to your right, then run down the side of the boat, out the back, and down the pier to the beach. As quietly as possible. Without getting caught."

She shook her head and shrugged. "Real simple."

"Yup." I grabbed her hand. I was scared we weren't going to get out of this, but there was no point in saying so. "Okay, let's go."

I crept to the door, Ginny glued to my back, and opened it. I peered down the hall. No one there. I motioned for her to go through. She did, and I followed her out. I pointed to the stairs, and she started that way. I paused when I heard scratching behind the opposite door.

Ginny frowned at me and mouthed, *What's wrong?*

More scratching, then a soft woof. I put my hand on the handle and slowly opened the door. A sturdy ball of fluff darted out and woofed at me while jumping on my legs. I picked the Welsh corgi up and cuddled his little head.

"Hello, Andi," a voice I recognized said from inside the room.

I stepped inside, holding Buttercup close to my chest. "Hello, Beatrice."

CHAPTER TWENTY-FOUR

"I'M IMPRESSED," BEATRICE SAID as she perched at the end of the bed in her expensive silk pajamas and house slippers. "I wondered if you would make the connection."

"I was surprised. I thought you were just a nice elderly lady unsure of what to do with the huge estate she'd inherited from her late husband. I'd never have guessed you were really a Russian mobster."

Beatrice chuckled. "Mobster is such a stupid word. I've never cared for it."

"How about gangster or criminal or... I know...*murderer*," I replied.

She sighed as she crossed her legs. "That was an unfortunate accident."

"Jeremy was bashed in the head and thrown off a cliff. Doesn't seem accidental."

"Well, he knew the risks when he stole money from us, and Ivan has no patience. Jeremy knew that, too," she replied.

Commotion in the corridor behind me made me turn. The aforementioned Ivan had Ginny, holding her by the upper arms, and she was struggling against him, but to no avail.

"Let Ginny go. She has no part in this," I said.

At first, I thought Beatrice was going to refuse, but her gaze went to Buttercup. I still held her firmly in my arms. Beatrice nodded and said, "Fine. Yes. But let's take this upstairs, shall we? I feel a bit claustrophobic with everyone crammed into my stateroom."

I backed out of the room, and Beatrice followed. I motioned for her to go first, and she did. She followed Ivan and Ginny up the stairs and into the main cabin. Like a gentleman, Victor stood as we all filed in. He wiped his mouth with a napkin and placed it onto the table next to his empty plate.

"I see we are all here now," he said with a chuckle.

"Beatrice said she would let Ginny go." I took a step away from Ivan. I didn't want him behind me. I stroked the dog's head. I would never hurt Buttercup, but Beatrice didn't know that for sure, and I needed leverage.

"Yes. Let Ginny go. We only needed her to get Andi here," Beatrice said as she sat on the sofa like a woman of leisure.

"That's right. I'm here, so Ginny goes."

Victor nodded to Ivan, who dropped his hands, releasing Ginny.

"Andi," Ginny whimpered.

"It's okay. Go, Ginny. Please."

She crossed the main cabin to the stern. There was a door that led out to the back deck and the dock. When she reached the door, she looked back at me.

I nodded at her. "I'll be okay. They just want the SIM card. Then they'll let me go."

I knew that wasn't true, but I had to make her leave or I wouldn't be able to keep up the façade.

She looked at the other faces, frowned, and then went out the door. I watched as she jumped over the rail and ran down the dock.

"Can I have Buttercup back now?" Beatrice asked with a humorous lift to her eyebrows.

I set the dog down, and he ran over to his owner, wagging his little butt. Beatrice patted the spot next to her on the sofa, and he jumped up and curled himself into a fuzzy ball.

"You better have that card on you," Victor said. "Would be a real shame to kill you now, after going to all this trouble."

"Of course, I do. But I know you're not going to let me go."

Beatrice blanched. "No? Why not?"

"Because I know too much." Victor gave a slight chin-lift toward Ivan. Ivan moved toward me as I backed up. "But you don't know who else has the bank account information. The printouts you grabbed aren't the only copies," I said in a jumbled rush.

Ivan stopped advancing. "If you mean your hotel buddy, Lane, I already snatched his computers. The storm was the perfect cover. His old-man roommate didn't even wake up."

Oops. My bluff's been called.

Ivan continued to advance.

"Okay!" I put my hand out. "I have the card, just give me a second." I patted the pockets of my jacket under my raincoat, trying to formulate a plan. "It's here somewhere." I reached into the pocket of the rain slicker, felt the butt of the taser gun. I wrapped my hand around the grip, hoping like hell that it was already loaded and ready to fire. I mentally smacked myself for not checking it before.

"Just grab her, Ivan," Beatrice said, "I'm tired and want to go home."

The moment he advanced toward me, another bolt of lightning lit up the sky, blinding everyone on the yacht. As the thunder cracked overhead, I turned and ran, hoping I was going in the right direction. All I could see were black spots.

I made it through the door, down the three steps, and vaulted over the railing like an Olympic hurdler. When my feet hit the dock, I ran as fast as I could, but not fast enough. Ivan snatched me by the back of my raincoat and yanked me toward him. The neckline choked me as I turned to face him.

I brought my hand out of my pocket and rammed the taser right against his chest.

Looking down between us, his eyes widened as I pressed the trigger. His whole body went rigid, and he vibrated violently, but he never lost his grip on me. I could feel the current over my hand, so I dropped the taser, releasing the trigger. Ivan sagged, wrapping his arms around me, and listed to the side, taking us both over the dock and into the churning water.

I heard someone scream my name as I sunk into the dark depths. But it must've been my own brain screaming at me. *Swim! Go up! Get to the surface! You'll die if you don't, Andi!*

I struggled, my arms and legs so heavy, so impossible to move. My lungs hurt like my chest was being crushed in a vise. I opened my eyes in the water, looking for a way out. Looking to save myself.

I saw a form in the water near me. A hulking dark form. It reached for me. I kicked at it. Flailed my hands at it. *Let me go!* I know I screamed that, because water filled my mouth.

Then the dark form was pulled back. Away from me, as if something had sucked it back with a powerful vacuum. I looked up, trying to see the surface, but everything was so black. So devoid of any life. I moved my arms, but I didn't go anywhere. I kicked with my legs, but I made no progress. It was like trying to ride a bike in spin class. Around and around, legs aching, pulsating with effort, but going nowhere.

This was it. This was the end. I couldn't fight anymore. I just wanted to sit back and relax.

Closing my eyes, I lowered my arms and let my body go. The cold around me hurt, clawing at my skin, piercing me with tiny shards of ice, but then a sudden warmth spread across me, and I smiled.

I'd finally found peace as the darkness swallowed me whole.

CHAPTER TWENTY-FIVE

ELECTRIC PAIN SHOT THROUGH my hands first. Then my feet, and then my nose. I peeled one eye open, and I was bouncing up and down. Everything was blurry and unidentifiable. Except I wasn't in the water anymore, fighting to breach the surface. I was on the beach, and I was being carried.

I tried to move my head, but whoever had me squeezed me tighter.

Then I heard a voice. "Andi!" It was Ginny.

I opened my eye again to see her face hovering over mine. Mascara streaked her face from her tears.

"Oh God, Andi." She touched my cheeks and then she looked over my head. "Is she going to be okay?"

"Let me put her down."

I was placed on a stone beach at the end of the dock, and several blankets were piled on top of me. Then another body pressed on top of me, rubbing at my arms. I opened both eyes and tried to smile as Luke massaged my arms and my hands.

"You're going to be okay, honey. You're going to be okay."

Then there was a lot of commotion around us. More blankets came. Two of them were wrapped around Luke, and I saw Deputy Marshall's face. He was shouting out orders to others around us. People I didn't recognize. The chaotic motions were too much for me, so I just concentrated on Luke's face. His beautiful face.

"I like your lips," I croaked, then I winced. My throat hurt, like I'd swallowed glass.

"I like yours, too," he said while he continued to rub my arms and hands. The pain was starting to fade.

I pursed my lips and tried to lift my head. He held me still, then leaned down and pressed his lips to mine. I couldn't feel them. I couldn't feel anything. Then everything went black.

When I woke again, I was in a hospital room. It was dark, but I could hear the beeping of machines hooked up to my body and the hum of the whole hospital coming through the vents. I tried to evaluate my body by starting with my toes, trying to wiggle them, and then tightening each muscle group all the way up to my face. I hurt, that was for sure. I had aches and pains in every nook and cranny.

Slowly, I turned my head. Next to the bed, slumped in a chair, eyes closed, was the sheriff. His hand was on the bed, hooked underneath mine. With everything I had, I moved my fingers and squeezed his hand.

He jerked awake, springing forward. He blinked rapidly, probably trying to clear his mind, and then he smiled at me. "You're awake."

I licked my lips and then whispered, "I think so."

"How do you feel?"

"Sore. Tired. Alive."

"Alive is good." He squeezed my hand.

I licked my lips again, and Luke grabbed the plastic water cup on the tray table. He brought the straw to my lips, and I sipped some water. It was room temperature, thank goodness. I didn't think I'd ever be able to drink cold water again without getting the shakes.

"So, did we get the bad guys?" I asked.

He nodded. "Yeah. We did."

"Good."

"The feds came in, and they took Victor and Beatrice into custody."

"What about Buttercup?"

His lips twitched upward. "Um, I believe Daisy has him in custody."

"Good. He's a sweet little dog. He shouldn't be punished for having a horrible owner." I could see in Luke's eyes that he was waiting for me to ask about Ivan. But I wasn't going to. I knew what had happened. I knew he was dead.

I shuffled a bit in the bed. My neck was starting to ache from turning and talking. Luke pushed the button that lifted the head of the bed, so I didn't have to move much to see him.

"How…how did you find me?"

"I figured something was going on, especially after I discovered you swiped the SIM card out of my pants pocket."

I refrained from smiling.

"I did a little more digging on the marina because you had been so adamant that Ivan had gone there. I found a registration under the name Beatrice Orlov for a boat. I checked that name and found it was the maiden name for Beatrice Sorokin. I discovered the boat had been moored there a few times. I knew the boat had to be somewhere." He kissed my hand and admitted, "Basically, Shawn told me he'd dropped you off at the stony beach dock."

"Wow, I can't believe Shawn did the exact opposite of what I thought he'd do."

He chuckled. "Yeah, go figure."

The door to my hospital room opened, and Ginny rushed in. Followed by the rest of the Park family: Lois, Eric, Nicole, and Samuel. Ginny came to the other side and literally tried to climb into the bed with me. Lois had to nudge her off.

"You'll crush her, Ginny."

With tears running down her face, Ginny grabbed my other hand and squeezed tightly. I didn't have the heart to tell her it hurt like hell. "You're okay. Right? You're okay?"

"I'm okay," I said.

Lois touched my foot through the blanket. "You saved our Ginny. We won't ever be able to thank you enough, Andi."

I looked at each of the Parks. I didn't know how to tell them that they had saved me years ago. They had given me the family I'd always dreamed of having. And in my neediest time, they had opened their arms to me without question and welcomed me home.

They had already thanked me in more ways than I could ever repay. Thinking of leaving them again to go to Hong Kong, after I'd just moved here from California, overwhelmed me with sadness. How could I possibly turn my back on them now?

CHAPTER TWENTY-SIX

I SETTLED THE LAST of my crime novels into the bookcase and took a step back to inspect my work. The empty cardboard box near my foot wriggled when Scout jumped into it. Jem joined her, and then it became a fight over who could fully occupy the inside and force the other one out. The struggle was real for a little while until they decided to call it a draw and curled up with each other, happily purring. They'd been purring a lot since I sprang them from Daisy's Pet Hotel.

Chuckling to myself, I turned and surveyed the living room. When she departed on her extended vacation, June had left all her furniture for me. Otherwise, the entire house would have been bare. The only things I'd added were my personal items, like pictures and candles, and my books. In time, I could add more.

It had been a week since the incident on the *Magpie*. A week since I'd nearly died. I only had to stay in the hospital for a couple of days, and then Ginny took me back to the Park and was determined to dote on me day and night. After the first day, I hated it and told her to stop. I loved her for the effort, though.

I had talked to the FBI while in the hospital. I told them everything I knew and handed over the SIM card, after the doctor cut the duct tape off my body. The duct tape had left several red lines on my belly. Lines that were still there. The doctor told me it wasn't necessarily the tape that scarred me, but the cold. Frostbite can be a strange thing. Thankfully, the frost didn't take any of my toes or fingers or nose. I'm not sure I could've handled that.

In the hospital, I had other visitors as well. Some of the staff from the hotel, like Tina and Nancy. Megan had come, bringing a new shirt for her dad, who hadn't left my side. Mayor Lindsey came with her husband, Justin. He brought me a whole cake. I devoured it in seconds while he stood there.

Lane had also come to see me. I apologized for getting him involved and for his computers being stolen. He said it wasn't a problem because he had a self-destruct mode on his hard drive. So, if anyone tried to log in, the drive would fry. He was really into some next-level spy kind of stuff that I really didn't want to know about. Besides that, he said, he had insurance and had already bought himself two new systems, even better than the stolen ones.

Before heading back to the mainland, Daniel also came by. Luke had left the room, giving us some privacy. Which was nice, although we really didn't have anything crucial to say to each other. I'd already told him that I had feelings for Luke. I just hadn't told Luke that, yet.

I picked up the teacup I'd set on June's coffee table and sipped the warm liquid on my way into the kitchen. I looked out the window into the back yard. I couldn't wait to sit outside in the morning and watch the sunrise. This house represented a lot of new beginnings for me. After months of being homeless and aimless, I was putting down roots. And it felt great.

There was a brief knock at the front door. Ginny came in carrying the last of my boxes. She set the box down in the living room, then bounced over to me and gave me a hug.

"Happy house warming," she said with a big smile.

"Aw, thank you."

She handed me a small, wrapped gift box. "Open it."

I tore off the paper and opened the case. It was a necklace. A gorgeous, dainty, silver chain with two silver cat charms on it.

"Oh, Ginny, I love it." She helped me put it on. I ran my hand over it, feeling tears welling in my eyes. "It's Scout and Jem."

"No, silly, it's you and me." She hugged me tight, and then she took out a stack of mail from her back pocket and handed it to me. "Oh yeah, here's your mail. It'll take a bit before everything gets forwarded to you here."

The door opened again, and Deputy Marshall brought in another of my boxes. "Where do you want this one?"

I pointed to the floor in the living room. "There's good. Thank you, Marshall."

"You're welcome." He looked down at the floor sheepishly.

"So, have a good time, and call me later." Ginny hugged me again. She met Marshall at the door, and he took her hand.

My eyes widened, but I didn't have a chance to say anything before they were walking down my lawn, hand in hand. I'd have to grill her later to find out when that had happened. Not that I thought her choice was a bad one. Clive Barrington wasn't a man who would have settled down with her here on the island. He'd have left her with a broken heart. Marshall was a sweet man, and

Ginny deserved sweet. He was the type who would cherish her, which was all I'd ever wanted for her. Ginny was the best and deserved just that.

I checked the time. I had about thirty minutes before my next visitor. Luke and I were going out on our first official date. I was both nervous and excited. I really didn't know what to expect. I mean, how does a man plan a date to top saving your life?

While I waited, I went through my mail. There was a mailer from JCPenney and my catalog from Victoria's Secret. Also, a couple letters from various charities that I'd contributed to in the past. And the last letter was from the State Bar of California.

I slid my thumb under the flap and tore open the envelope. My hands shook as I took out the paper and unfolded it. I read it, my eyes resting on each word. My law license had been cleared. I could now practice law in California. I could be a lawyer again.

The front door opened, and Luke walked in. Every inch of him was desirable. The way his dark hair was slicked back but still looked like he'd been running his hands through it. His faded blue jeans that fit him snug in all the right places. The burgundy shirt that made his fierce blue eyes pop. He'd shaved, and his cologne made the saliva pool in my mouth. He was simply devastating to look at.

"Hey," he said. "You about ready to go?"

I still held the letter as I nodded.

He glanced at it, then my face. "Everything okay?"

"Everything's exactly as it should be." I folded the letter, stuffed it back into the envelope, and tossed it on the table.

I met him at the door.

"So," he started, "I thought we could eat—"

I took his face in my hands and kissed him properly for the first time.

The kiss was everything I imagined it would be. Soft, gentle, loving. I felt it from the top of my head to the tips of my toes, and everywhere in between. Then he wrapped a hand in my hair and deepened the kiss until I could no longer think.

When we broke apart, I was breathless, my head spinning. "How about we eat in, instead." I nipped at his chin.

"I like how you think, Ms. Steele." He reached down, put an arm under my legs, and swept me up into his arms to carry me away.

Ginny had been right all along. The sheriff was most definitely a sweeper.

ABOUT THE AUTHOR

Diane Capri is an award-winning *New York Times*, *USA Today*, and world-wide bestselling author. She writes several series, including the Park Hotel Mysteries, the Hunt for Justice, Hunt for Jack Reacher, and Heir Hunter series, and the Jess Kimball Thrillers. She's a recovering lawyer and snowbird who divides her time between Florida and Michigan. An active member of Mystery Writers of America, Author's Guild, International Thriller Writers, Alliance of Independent Authors, and Sisters in Crime, she loves to hear from readers and is hard at work on her next novel.

Please connect with her online:

http://www.DianeCapri.com

Twitter: http://twitter.com/@DianeCapri

Facebook: http://www.facebook.com/Diane.Capri1

http://www.facebook.com/DianeCapriBooks

Made in the USA
Monee, IL
03 May 2022